Meeting Eternity
The Sullivan Vampires, Volume 1

Bridget Essex

Meeting Eternity

Other Books by Bridget Essex

Raised by Wolves
Wolf Heart
Wolf Queen
Falling for Summer
The Guardian Angel
The Vampire Next Door (with Natalie Vivien)
A Wolf for Valentine's Day
A Wolf for the Holidays
The Christmas Wolf
Don't Say Goodbye
Forever and a Knight
A Knight to Remember
Date Knight
Wolf Town
Dark Angel
Big, Bad Wolf

Erotica

Wild
Come Home, I Need You

Meeting Eternity

About the Author

My name is Bridget Essex, and I've been writing about vampires for almost two decades. I'm influenced most by classic vampires– the vision of CARMILLA (it's one of the oldest lesbian novels!) and DRACULA. My vampires have always been kind of traditional (powerful), but with the added self-torture of regret and the human touch of guilt.

I have a vast collection of knitting needles and teacups, and like to listen to classical music when I write. My first date with my wife was strolling in a garden, so it's safe to say I'm a bit old fashioned. I have a black cat I love very much, and two white dogs who actually convince me to go outside. When I'm actually outside, I begin to realize that writing isn't all there is to life. Just most of it! I'm married to the love of my life, author Natalie Vivien.

The love story of the beautiful but tragic vampire Kane Sullivan and her sweetheart Rose Clyde is my magnum opus, and I'm thrilled to share it with you in *The Sullivan Vampires* series, published by **Rose and Star Press**! Find out more at www.LesbianRomance.org and http://BridgetEssex.Wordpress.com

Meeting Eternity: The Sullivan Vampires, Volume 1
Copyright © 2016 Bridget Essex - All Rights Reserved
Published by Rose and Star Press
First edition, February 2016

This is a work of fiction. Names, characters, places and incidents either are products of the author's imagination or are used fictitiously. Any resemblance to actual events or locales or persons, living or dead, is entirely coincidental.

This book, or parts thereof, may not be reproduced without written permission.

ISBN: 1530201810
ISBN-13: 978-1530201815

MEETING ETERNITY

Meeting Eternity

DEDICATION

For the love of my life.

And for R.M., who knows, loves and appreciates the vampire gene better than anyone else. Thank you for knowing I could do it. This one's for you.

Meeting Eternity

-- Eternal Hotel --

The first time I saw Kane Sullivan, she saved my life.

The second time I saw her, I died.

That was the thing about Kane. Every moment around her was life and death, seconds and decisions that could never be predicted. But even after all of that, even after all of this time, I can still say that she was worth it.

This is the story of why she was worth it all.

My life before working at the Sullivan Hotel was a sad blur. My long-term girlfriend, Anna, and I had been together for two years. I loved her. I thought we were going to be together forever. But one night, on the way back from the grocery store, her bicycle was hit by a drunk driver, and in a heartbeat, my life was changed forever.

I don't remember much about the months after Anna died. I suppose that I got up as I always did, got dressed in my green apron and walked the two blocks to the little boutique grocery store, Rosa's, on the upscale side of town where I worked. I would go through my shift as their produce manager, which involved a lot of ordering different vegetables, arranging them in pretty, enticing rows and disposing of the rotting ones. After my shift, I'd come home, back to my too-empty apartment with a bag of slightly wilted vegetables that were still edible, but now too ugly to sell. I'd go through the motions of making dinner, of forcing myself to eat it. I'd curl up on the bed. Our bed. And I'd cry myself to sleep.

I did that for six months, but I don't remember hardly any of it.

I'd ask myself on really hard nights, nights when I wondered where my life was going, what I was doing with it, how this had all happened, this radical departure from how I'd assumed life was *supposed* to be. On the darkest, hardest nights, I wondered if I'd really loved Anna. The thing is, I knew I'd loved her. I'd loved her deeply. I'd been hoping to spend the rest of my life with her. But in the really terrible moments of weeping over the spaghetti at the now too-big kitchen table, far too big for only one person, I wondered if—when Anna died—she'd taken the best parts of my life with her.

That's the thing. Without Anna, I was just Rose Clyde. Boring Rose Clyde who wore her boring red hair in the same ponytail since high school. Who had worked at Rosa's since I'd graduated from college. I was a produce manager with a useless bachelor's in art history. I had no dreams, no aspirations. It was pathetic. *I* was pathetic. Life had come up too fast and too quickly, and it had hit me broadside. Part of me thought that I was still in college, dreaming of the time that I'd graduate, that I'd do something exciting with my degree, perhaps move to New York and work in a museum finding interesting and beautiful new discoveries from famous painters. That I'd change the world, if only a little. But I was never going to change my life that drastically. I was never going to move to New York. *Brave* people moved to New York.

And I'd never been brave.

I'd lived in Greensprings all my life. Greensprings is in New Hampshire, close to the border of Massachusetts, and it's very beautiful here. But it's a town that people drive through on their way to more beautiful and more interesting locations. No one knows where Greensprings actually is and no one sets out to find it. It's one of those very quaint towns that on television, people set wacky sitcoms in, and growing up, I'd had more fantasies that I'd get a condo in the upscale part of it, live a bohemian lifestyle that involved a lot of painting and wine and women. But I couldn't paint. And before Anna, I couldn't keep a girlfriend to save my life.

I was pretty good at the wine part.

Sometimes I hated how boring I was, making my safe decisions that meant that I'd lived in Greensprings all my life, that I would *continue* to live in Greensprings probably until the day I'd die. Anna was going to change that. She'd wanted to move to New York, too, and we'd been saving money together for just that purpose. We were going to move together, rent a probably much-too-small apartment and then...we didn't know. But we often talked about that dream long into the night. Let's be honest: it was mostly Anna's dream. But I was so happy, so glad to go along with it. Anna had that way about her. A big, wide smile and twinkling brown eyes that promised that if you'd trust her, everything was going to be all right in the end.

But Anna was dead now. And everything was most certainly not all right.

I knew that I was spiraling into a depression that I might not ever recover from, but I didn't know how to stop it. I didn't know if I even wanted to stop it. What was my life without Anna?

And then, one day, Gwen called.

I hadn't seen Gwen since the funeral. My best friend since college, Gwen was always the brave one, the one who took risks, went to exotic, daring places. When I saw her name on my cell phone's caller ID, I wondered, as I pressed the phone to my ear, where she'd be calling me from. With Gwen, you could never be sure if she was down the street, in another country, or even on this planet (she'd reminded me more than once on an all-night cramming session in school that someday they'd probably sell seats on a rocket to the moon: and she'd be first in line to buy a ticket. I didn't doubt that for a second).

"Hi, honey!" Gwen said, the line crackling with all the static of a terrible connection. "Honey, it's been forever: how *are* you?"

Oh, that question. People ask you that question all the time, but they don't really want to hear the real answer—they're just doing it because it's something we're taught to say. Every day, regulars at the grocery store would brush past me in the aisle to get their stalks of brussels sprouts and their kohlrabi, and they'd ask me that question. And if I broke down, if I told them that I was doing terribly, that my girlfriend had been hit by a drunk driver and died and I was falling to pieces because of it, they'd back away slowly, maybe never come back to the grocery store again. So I always lied to them, told them I was "fine." They didn't really want to know how I was doing. Few people in the world cared enough for the truth.

But Gwen did.

I broke down, trying to keep the majority of my tears in check, but she heard my little hiccup-sob on the other end of the line, even over all of the static, and she made a little gasp of her own.

"Oh, honey, I'm so sorry," said Gwen, and I knew that she meant every word of it. "Please don't cry. I'm so sorry. Is it really bad? You're not even a little okay?"

No. I wasn't. I was falling to pieces. I took a deep breath, the sound of it catching in the back of my throat as I grappled with words, trying to figure out what exactly I could tell Gwen that would convey...everything.

"Things are pretty bad," is what I settled on, then. It wasn't much, but it was all I could say as I wrestled with the tears and the sobs, trying to keep the last bits of myself together. And failing.

"I wish so much that I could be there right now. You don't know how much I wish that," she said softly, her words as soothing as a cool cloth to my forehead. I sighed, holding the cell phone tightly to my ear, like a lifeline thrown to a drowning man at sea. "That's...actually the reason that I'm calling, honey," she said then. The words were still sincere, still soft and gentle. But they were beginning to take on a slightly wheedling quality that made me blink.

Gwen wanted something.

"What is it?" I managed, taking another tissue out of one of the ten tissue boxes on the coffee table, wiping my nose, my eyes, my face. I crumpled the tissue in my hand as silence continued on the other end of the line. Until:

"I want you to come to Maine."

They were absolutely crazy words, but she'd said them so sincerely, one might almost have taken her seriously. I snorted into the phone, lying back against our couch. My couch. I tried to swallow the sob that escaped my throat, then, but didn't quite manage.

"Look, I know you're going through a really tough patch right now. But you and I both know that there's nothing in Greensprings to keep you there, and to be perfectly honest, I think a change in scenery would be *really* good for you. I read a book about grieving—you know the one I recommended you that you wouldn't read? It said that getting out of your usual patterns will help you make some sense of the tragedy, might help you get back to living your life—"

I would never be able to make *any* sense of the tragedy. And I was honestly uncertain if there was any life to get back to living. I was shaking my head, wanted to change the subject, but she couldn't hear that on the other end of the line. So I said, clearing my throat: "What are you doing in Maine?"

Gwen snorted a little. "Haven't you been reading *any* of my emails?"

I stared at the laptop on the kitchen table, untouched for weeks. "No," I sighed truthfully.

"I got a new job," said Gwen then, her voice dropping a little in excitement, as if she was telling me a secret. "Rose, it's the best job I've *ever had*. It's unreal. I'm working at this old hotel in a really cute little town—it's right on the ocean. In *Maine*! It looks like an old black and white movie should be set here, seriously. The hotel is this gorgeous old building right on a cliff face overlooking the water—it's just too pretty for words. I keep thinking I'm going to run into Scarlet O'Hara or the Queen of England or something in the hallways, and—"

"Wait, wait, wait," I finally managed, holding up my hand that clutched the tissue. "What are you doing working in a hotel?"

"I work the front desk. It's the easiest job in the world. The hotel's kind of in an out-of-the-way town, and—"

"Where is it?"

"In Maine, silly! I just said, and—"

"Where in Maine?" I persisted.

"It's kind of a stupid name for a town," said Gwen with a little laugh. "It sounds like a soap opera should be set here. Or a horror movie. It doesn't sound real. But the hotel is in Eternal Cove."

Eternal Cove. She was right. It *didn't* sound real. But when Gwen said those words, a little chill ran through me—the kind that made the hairs on my arms stand up, my shoulders giving a little shake of their own accord. My mother used to say that this was the kind of feeling you got when someone walked over your grave. I never knew exactly what she meant by that. I wasn't dead yet. I didn't even have a grave. But there was such an odd chill that moved through me in that moment, it felt as if I did have a grave. And someone had very deliberately waltzed over the top of it.

"Huh," was the dubious response I gave into the phone.

"The thing is, the place is normally completely dead, so not that much help is needed, even though the hotel is huge. Because, really, we maybe get like a guest a week. But there's some conference or other that's coming to Eternal Cove this next month....October," said Gwen. On the other end of the line, I could hear her shuffling through some papers. "And my boss needs to take on a few more staff, she tells me. And she asked me if I could recommend anyone to her, and I..." There was a very long sigh through the phone. "To be honest, I recommended you."

"What?" The floor began to reel beneath me. "But I...I already have a job. I work at Rosa's," I spluttered. There were so many reasons why this was ludicrous, I almost didn't even know where to begin. "Gwen, I mean, I've worked at Rosa's for over ten years, and..."

"*And?* It's a grocery store, Rose. You're not exactly on the fast track to success at a grocery store." She didn't mean to sound condescending, but it came out that way, regardless.

"That's rotten. You know that's rotten," I told her softly. A snort came from the other end of the phone.

"Honey, if I don't tell you this, *no one's* going to tell you this. So it's sort of my duty as your best friend to tell you that if you, Rose Clyde, don't leave Greensprings now? You're never going to leave it. You're going to stay there forever with your grief." She said these words gently, but there was a hard edge to the last few of them. "I know Anna's death was very, very hard on you, and I'm so sorry. But it's been six months. Anna died. You didn't. You've got to keep living, honey. You've got to decide that you want to keep living, and you've got to make that decision now." There was a long pause, and then she finally said, simply: "Anna wouldn't have wanted this for you, honey. All Anna ever wanted was for you to be happy."

I didn't know what to say. So I said nothing. After another long moment of silence, Gwen sighed again. "Look, it's the easiest job in the world. It's such a beautiful town. I know your apartment's lease is on a month-to-month basis, so that would be insanely easy to get out of. I know that if you absolutely hated it here in Eternal Cove and you went back to Greensprings, Rosa's would take you back in a heartbeat, so that's insanely easy, too. Rose, honey, you have absolutely, positively nothing to lose, and pretty much everything to gain. And I could help you get through the rough spots, get you to start living again. Aaaaand..." She trailed off, her voice dropping to a whisper again. "I wasn't going to bring it up, but I'm pulling out the big guns of convincing here." She cleared her throat, and I could hear her smile through the phone. "If you ever *are* ready again, for...well. I just want you to know that there are some *ridiculously* gorgeous ladies here."

I couldn't believe she'd just said that. It had only been *six months*. And I was fairly certain that I was never going to date anyone else *ever again*. But as I opened my mouth to tell her "no," that the whole thing was a terrible, no-good, rotten bad idea, I took a deep breath.

I looked up.

I looked up at the apartment. At what had been *our* apartment. Every last thing here reminded me of Anna. The now-empty peg on the wall by the door where she'd hung her jean jacket. Her set of car keys with the ridiculous Pooh Bear keychain, sitting in the pottery bowl by the door. Her old plaid work shirt that she'd left on the counter the night of the accident that I'd never had the heart to move. I knew what I was doing, had done, to the place where we'd lived: I'd turned it into a shrine to Anna. I was never going to move on with my life while living here.

I knew that.

And Gwen knew that, too.

"Please," said Gwen, quietly. Softly. "Please, Rose. Give this a chance."

I couldn't believe it when I said it. But I'd said it, and there was no going back now:

I whispered, simply: "Okay."

Gwen made the drive that weekend to Greensprings. When she arrived in the parking lot, all but beaching her old, beat-up blue van that she'd dubbed Moochie in the edge of the lot by the bushes, I ran out to meet her, and we hugged for about five minutes, both of us crying. Gwen had an equally useless degree in theater, and we'd been through so much together in college and beyond it, had been there for each other through everything. And now, again, our lives were changing. But at least we were changing together.

She helped me box up the apartment, making piles of things. There was a "keep" pile, a "discard" pile, and a "donate" pile. The "donate" pile was the biggest as we went through each room of the apartment. We hadn't had that much stuff, Anna and I, and Anna's mother had taken a few boxes of her daughter's belongings after the funeral, but there was still, surprisingly, a lot of things. There were times that I broke down crying, drawing my knees up as I sat on the living room floor, Gwen rubbing little circles on my back and making trips to the local liquor store for really cheap wine. But somehow, miraculously, in two days we got through it.

And I ended up with a single suitcase of clothes, and a few plastic totes of things. That was it. That was, somehow, my life's worth of possessions.

It made me feel sad and small. And completely alone.

But Gwen wouldn't let me feel that way for long. She drove me to my apartment manager's office, and I told the woman I'd vacated the apartment.

And then that was it. It was over.

I walked through the apartment one last time, running my fingers over the counter that Anna had pressed me against when she wanted to kiss me deeply, putting her hands into the back pockets of my jeans as she held me to her. I was leaving the couch behind, the couch that had held us both as we watched movies together, me sitting in her lap as she held me tightly around the waist. My eyes filled with tears as I walked through every small room, and I said goodbye for the last time. Even if I moved back, I'd never have this apartment again.

But a still, small voice in the back of my head—or maybe my heart—knew the truth of it. I was never coming back to Greensprings again.

I couldn't.

"I'm turning into you," I told Gwen when I climbed up into the passenger side of Moochie, her van. Gwen cast me a sidelong grin as she turned the key in the ignition. She was looking exceptionally eccentric today, her long, frizzy brown hair in two braids falling down her back over the paisley peasant blouse. Her blue eyes flashed as she winked at me, Moochie roaring to life beneath her hands.

"You mean you're becoming reckless?" She grinned, casting a glance over her shoulder as she

21

backed out of the parking space.

"I'm becoming crazy," I muttered, fingers sinking into the plush arms of my seat as Gwen roared out of the parking lot, narrowly avoiding a truck that honked for about five minutes behind us irately.

"Crazy's good!" she yelled over the boom of the engine. "A crazy person has adventures, sees amazing things…has a good life," she said a little softer, but I still heard it.

I wanted to have a good life. Doesn't everyone? I just thought that particular ship had already sailed for me. That my chance of having a good life died with Anna.

But maybe not. Maybe in this absolutely crazy move, I'd been given another chance. Another chance in Eternal Cove. I put my chin in my hand and watched the just-turning trees race past our window in red and golden blurs as Gwen weaved in and out of country roads and little roads and bigger roads on our way through New Hampshire toward Maine.

"What kind of person just takes your word for it when hiring someone?" I asked Gwen what was probably a very obvious question, but one I hadn't yet considered as we paused at a fast food joint, stretching as we tumbled out of the van. "The owner of Eternal Cove didn't even want a resume you said…" I muttered, patting my jacket pocket to make certain my wallet was still in it. It was.

"I dunno," said Gwen, shrugging and touching her toes, which caused a group of college boys to run into a garbage can as they walked past, not looking where they were going. I stared at them with a frown, but they weren't exactly looking at me, either. Even though Gwen was about fifteen years their senior, she had that sort of quality about her. She could have charmed the antlers off of a moose. "She just asked me who she should hire for the job, I told her about you, and she said you were hired if you wanted it," she grinned, stretching overhead and straightening.

"That just seems odd—no resumes, no interviews," I muttered, following Gwen and the scent of french fries through the door and into the ordering line. Gwen shoved her hands into the pockets of her coat, shrugged.

"I mean, she's eccentric," said Gwen, peering up at the lit menu above us, glowing with tantalizing pictures of sandwiches and beverages. "Do I want a number five or a number seven?"

"Five," I said glancing up. "What do you mean, 'eccentric'?"

"I'd like a number five, please!" Gwen told the fast food attendant cheerfully. "And if you could give me that in the largest size possible, I'd greatly appreciate it." She pulled a couple of bills out of her pocket and shrugged at me. "I mean *eccentric*," she muttered, taking the receipt with her order number.

"And for you?" the fast food guy said in a very bored tone of voice.

"Um…a medium coffee and a large order of fries, thanks," I said, handing him my debit card. He swiped it through and gave me my receipt, and I followed Gwen to the side where we waited with a bunch of other hungry-looking people for our orders. "You're being dodgy," I told her then with a frown.

"I mean, she's kind of quiet. Keeps to herself. Wears a suit and tie…" said Gwen, trailing off and watching me closely for a reaction. "That's why I told you about the whole 'gorgeous women' thing. I'm pretty sure my boss is gay. And a few other people there are, too, I think."

"How is that even possible? It's a little town in Maine…how many lesbians can there possibly be? And if you think she's gay just because she wears a tie, your gaydar is massively malfunctioning," I snorted, not caring that the elderly man ahead of us was frowning with all of his might back at me.

"My gaydar is functioning just fine, thanks. And I wasn't talking about lesbians in the town…I mean, there might be. I was actually talking about just in the hotel," said Gwen mildly, biting her lip. "Um…"

"Order seventy-nine!" yelled one of the attendants, dropping a tray of very largely sized bags on the counter.

"That's me!" said Gwen with glee, stepping forward and scooping up the bags.

"Order eighty!" It took me a second to process that this was my order. Mostly because I was trying to compute the fact that there was a hotel apparently full of gay women in Maine.

"I mean, not everyone there's gay, I don't think," said Gwen, bursting my bubble as we headed back to the car. "I mean, I'm not. I think the head cook isn't. But my gaydar has gone off every single time I meet anyone new from the Sullivan clan, and—"

"Whoa, whoa, whoa…back up there. I think you need to tell me the whole story. From the *beginning*."

We headed back to the van with bags of more calories than ten people should probably have ingested for lunch and very large cups of coffee. The scent of the french fries mixed with the steam from the coffee made my stomach roar in protest, begging to be fed.

"So the Sullivan Hotel is the only hotel or motel or whatever in Eternal Cove," said Gwen, starting the engine again. "You're going to love Eternal Cove, by the way. It's this crazy little town. Everyone I've met is awesome, and there's this cute little clothing boutique, and... Anyway," she continued, when she caught my glance. "The hotel is owned by Kane Sullivan. She's going to be your new boss. And she has a pretty big family. They all live at the hotel."

"Big family?" I dipped a french fry into the hole on the top of my cup of coffee and took a bite.

"That's disgusting," said Gwen, wrinkling her nose as she took a chug of coffee. "And yeah, big family. I guess she had a lot of adopted sisters? Or something? Look, I don't try to be nosy, but there are a lot of ladies who are staying at the hotel, all with the last name of Sullivan. And they don't *look* related. It's kind of weird, but they're all nice to me, so I've never really pried, asked questions, you know? Anyway, if you ask me, I kind of think maybe all of those ladies are her harem or something," she said, waggling her eyebrows at me as she took another sip of coffee. "They're all really unspeakably gorgeous, all of the women I've met. And they cover the whole spectrum of gay ladies, apparently. I've met butches and femmes and really hard femmes, and...I'm telling you, I genuinely think all of those women are her harem."

"Get your mind out of the gutter," I snorted, rolling my eyes as I dipped another french fry in my coffee as I tried to wrap my head around this. Gorgeous lesbian women. All with the same last name, living in an old hotel. It was a *little* weird. "And french fries in coffee isn't disgusting," I told her proudly as she made a little sound. "It's actually quite tasty. Tell me a little more about Kane..." I said then, sitting back in my seat and cradling my coffee cup in my hands. Kane Sullivan. What kind of a name was Kane?

"Like I said, she's a little weird. But she's always been really nice to me. She's very quiet, but when she comes into a room..." Gwen actually shivered when she said those words, her shoulders shaking a little as she breathed out. "I mean, you know it when she walks through a door, is all," she said, raising her eyebrows at me. "She has this...presence. It's really commanding. I hope you know it took quite a bit of courage from me to tell her about you. I had to seek her out, ask her for a meeting. I told her about you, and she just said you were hired if you wanted the job. She makes very firm, very quick decisions. She's just...that kind of lady. "

"You mean an eccentric lady," I said, holding my cup a little tighter as the sun came out from behind the clouds, causing all of the trees to brighten, their leaves moving in the wind, as red as if they were on fire.

"Yeah," said Gwen, though her brows had risen a little higher.

We drove a little farther in silence. Her eating the contents of her greasy paper bags of fast food. Me munching on french fries soggy with coffee, thinking about how absolutely crazy I was to have gone along with this.

The sun lit up the autumn trees, the road stretching ahead of us leading toward the unknown.

When we passed the town sign for "Eternal Cove, a Pleasant Place to Live!" it was already dark out.

The spotlight trained on the town sign was much too bright, and the faded quality of its paint was more visible than anyone would have probably liked. There was a little graphic sun over a few faded blue waves next to "Eternal Cove." We'd been able to smell the salt air for a few miles coming in through the van's vents, but it was too dark to make out the water that Gwen assured me was on my right. Occasionally, I saw a flashing light, far out into the blackness, that I assumed was a passing boat.

The air felt like a storm was coming, and the sky was as dark as a grave.

We drove down the small main street of Eternal Cove. Old Victorian buildings that looked a little run down held a tea house, a coffee shop, a Subway restaurant, a Chinese place, a barber shop and an antique store that had a slightly horrifying mannequin in the front window wearing a clown mask surrounded by orange lights. It was finally October, and there were pumpkins and sagging cornstalks tied to each lamppost along the way. The street was almost completely deserted, although my watch told me that it was only eight o'clock-ish on a Sunday night.

"They close up early around here," said Gwen with a shrug as the van's blunt nose began to edge upwards. We'd gone through the main street, and now we were winding our way up what must be a very impressive hill. I peered out of the window, up and up, wishing that it was still daylight so that I could see.

"You'll get to see it tomorrow," Gwen promised, her grin infectious as she turned the van along a looping curve of the road, her knuckles white on the worn wheel. "The Sullivan Hotel is *really* impressive in the daylight, but I honestly think you'll be pretty impressed by it at night, too..."

We rounded a bend in the road, and then there it was.

The Sullivan Hotel.

I'm pretty certain my jaw hit the floor of the van.

I was reminded, instantly, of the kind of period dramas they show on PBS. The Sullivan Hotel looked like it belonged in England...not here. Not in Maine, US of A. It was this sprawling, monstrously huge blocky building, seven stories high, with columns and towers. But the very first thing I noticed about it was the color of stone it was made out of. I supposed I'd seen red stone buildings before, but they'd never stuck out in my mind. Maybe because they weren't *this* red. The building was a color of red that you should only call "blood." And, to top it all off, almost every room throughout its monstrous sprawl of rooms was lit like it was on fire. That's the impression that I got, actually—that the entire building was on fire, but it was made of stone—very red stone—so that'd be impossible. But still...it seemed to flicker, even when I closed my eyes. The Sullivan Hotel burned itself in my vision, *even when I closed my eyes*.

I suppose that maybe I should have been afraid of it, a big red building outside of town, lit up and flickering like a bad omen. Gwen parked Moochie along the front walkway, and we both got out of the van, staring up and up and up at the sprawling building. It was lavish, excessive. Beautiful. With all of its columns and towers and—as I peered up, I noticed at the very top over the front door—gargoyles. Gwen glanced eagerly at me before opening up the van's side door and lugging out my suitcase.

"Come on, I can't wait to show you—" She kept talking, but she was trotting ahead of me, just a little too far for me to hear, and I had to almost run to keep up, picking up and lurching along with my suitcase so that it banged against my thigh as we walked up the shallow stone steps toward the entrance. The Sullivan Hotel's main entrance had four massive marble pillars pockmarked by the salty Maine rain (I didn't even *know* that marble came in red), and scarlet planters on either side of each pillar big enough to contain a body. Not that I immediately thought that when looking at them, but there was something about this entryway that made my thoughts turn a little ghastly. Maybe it was the tiny, carved red faces on the planters—gargoyle faces. Spooky faces with distended tongues, bulging eyes and curving horns. I shuddered a little as Gwen held open the main door for me, a big wooden thing that it took her two hands to keep steady and open. I stepped through, and then it was over. I'd made my decision fully, for better or worse.

I was here.

I had entered the Sullivan Hotel, and my choice was made.

Dark oak paneling along the cathedral-height walls echoed back the sound of my flats on the checkerboard floor, a checkerboard made not of the usual white and black squares, but of red and black. Together, Gwen and I walked toward the front desk, a big sprawling wooden thing carved with loops and filigree that looked wide enough to park a carriage on (my brain was thinking in Victorian pictures at this point—the hotel did that to you), much too wide for what I assumed was the guest book, the old leather thing cracked open to two empty cream pages. The antique brass bell on the counter made a tinny *ding!* when Gwen pressed her palm to it, and the sound carried down the hallway, around the corner...maybe it went on forever.

Two massive corridors, big enough to drive a couple of semis down at the same time, stretched away to our left and to our right. But right to the side of the old oaken desk rose a stairway. I guess I'd been expecting something impressive, something Queen Victoria would have walked down. But this staircase was actually not like the corridors at all, not like the impressive desk or the rising cathedral ceilings around us. The staircase was a tall, spindly thing, much too wide, but also as steep as a cliff face. It didn't look like steps, but rather like a ladder had been propped against one of the walls. I stared up at it in shock, the dark wood contrasting with the red of the carpeting on the steps. It looked like a tongue.

"We don't usually use that staircase," said Gwen, wrinkling her nose as she followed my gaze. When she caught my expression she chuckled a little and wiggled her fingers at me, eyes wide. "They say a couple of people have fallen to their deaths on that staircase! We call it the Widowmaker."

"Great," I muttered, setting the suitcase down beside my foot, shivering a little.

There were paintings on the walls here, old paintings that I realized—a little shocked—were originals. I wandered over to the closest one. It was of a naked woman, lounging on a rock, her back to the viewer, her face in profile as she turned, gazing to the left. She had long, straight blonde hair, a full mouth and flashing blue eyes, and she was smiling, amused, as she gazed regally at a big black cat that reminded me of a lion more than a panther as it crouched along the edge of the painting. But it wasn't the cat that the viewer's eyes were drawn to. It was the woman. She looked regal, powerful, and I felt the skin on my arms begin a shiver. I liked the painting very much, but it reminded me of something. It reminded me of...

"Earth to Rose, come in Rose!" Gwen joked, touching my arm lightly. "It says on the sheet here that I'm supposed to cover the front desk tonight so...I guess I'll show you to your room, and then I've got duty!"

"So no one was covering the front desk?" I said, bewildered, blinking and staring back at the big oaken desk, utterly empty. "That doesn't make any sense. What if someone came in?"

"Oh, no one really comes to Eternal Cove," said Gwen, wrinkling her nose. "Come on! This way!"

"A hotel that no one visits. So bizarre," I muttered, hefting up my suitcase again and turning to follow her down the broad hallway, the unnerving red and black checkerboard pattern of the floor continuing on under my feet. I paused as I passed the painting again, my gaze lingering on the woman's commanding presence, her long blonde hair flowing over her shoulders and back, the way her smile curved. It was a courageous smile. She wasn't afraid of that beast. Strangely, I got the feeling that it's almost as if she'd summoned it to her.

"Rose!"

"I'm coming..." I said, and then I was, trotting down the hallway at a brisk clip, and around the corner, following Gwen. The skin on my arms pricked as I continued along the curve of the hall, as the paintings, all with little lamps overhead like you'd see in a private gallery, lit and showcasing the works of art in their full glory, continued on and on, all different subjects and artistic styles and time periods.

Here was a painting done in the impressionistic style, similar to Monet, but this was no charming idyll with water lilies and bridges over duck ponds. This was an impressionistic painting of a skull, all dashes of white and muddied browns in thick globs of paint. I didn't like it even a little bit. Here was another painting, done in a cubist style—all long angles and bright, garish oranges and reds—of a cup of orange water. Again, it didn't suit my tastes, though I know that all art is subjective. Gwen was too far ahead down the looping, turning corridors for me to even see her at this point, and there weren't any doors off of the corridor—it's as if the hallway was built specifically to showcase the art.

It's as if the hallway went on forever.

I paused, then, paused because I couldn't bear the feeling anymore. You know the feeling. The pricking sensation on the back of your neck, the hair on your arms rising. The feeling you get when you're being watched. I turned, but I was in a peculiar place in the corridor, a little bend where I couldn't see the hallway curve ahead of me or behind me. My skirts swished around me as my suitcase turned with my upper body. I glanced back.

But there was no one there.

"Come *on*, Rose!" echoed the far-off sounding voice of Gwen, somewhere down the corridor.

"Coming!" I called back, trotting down the hall with my chin over my shoulder, still glancing back. Even though I moved down the corridor, even though I moved past remarkable paintings, the hall turning and twisting under my feet with the odd red and black checkerboard of marble, even though I saw not a single other soul than the occasional back of Gwen...I still couldn't shake the feeling of eyes on me.

Maybe it was just me. I was tired—we'd been driving for most of the day, and I was never much for road trips. Eternal Cove was farther up the Maine coastline than I'd thought. I'd just uprooted my entire life, had given up the apartment I'd had for years, had given up the job that was familiar, that had somehow become a part of me. Of course I'd be feeling a little uneasy. I was still wondering if all of this was a good idea. Yes. That was it. I was just uneasy about the changes, the *massive* life changes I'd just undergone. But as I kept walking down the hallway, I'd glance over my shoulder every now and again, the hairs on the back of my neck pricking up, still unable to completely shake the feeling that there was someone back there, watching me.

But there was never anyone there.

"I know this seems like a long way," said Gwen, her hand on a spiral staircase as I rounded the final corner of the corridor. The staircase was a dark mahogany, and seemed very old. It was ornate, carved with little vines and leaves and stylized filigree. "But, seriously." Gwen wrinkled her nose. "You don't want to go up that main set of stairs. They don't call it the 'Widowmaker' for nothing."

"They've not heard of elevators, then?" I joked with a grin as we both began to climb the wide spiral steps, Gwen's fingers trailing along the banister, and me clutching and lugging up my now overly heavy suitcase.

"This place is too old for that," said Gwen with a wink as we reached the first landing. "Anyway, this is the second floor," she said, gesturing with her hand down the long hallway. It looked like any hallway in a nice, older hotel—the plush red carpet stretching along a well-lit corridor that sported wallpaper covered in little golden blossoms and ornate golden light fixtures that drooped from overhead like wilting flowers.

"These are the rooms for the guests, when we have them." Gwen pointed upward. "The old servants' quarters are up on the fifth floor, and that's where the employees live now. Not much has changed in like...two hundred years."

"Great," I muttered, following her up to the second level. And then the third and fourth. By the fourth landing, I was wondering if I could make it, and—mercifully—Gwen grabbed my suitcase and lugged it up the final set of steps for me.

"It gets easier after you go up and down these a few thousand times. That's why my legs are looking so good," she quipped as we reached the blessed final landing. "You didn't say my legs were looking great when you saw me, by the way."

"They're great," I panted as we began down the wide hallway. There were large oaken doors every twenty feet or so on either side, their doorframes painted different colors, which looked out of place and interesting in such old surroundings. We passed a red doorframe, a blue doorframe, a pink doorframe...

"You're green," Gwen informed me, nodding to the fourth door on the right. It had a bright green doorframe, the color of green that usually was reserved for bottles of poison and rivers of acid. I grimaced as she took out an old skeleton key from her pocket and handed it to me. The slim brassy bit of metal looked like it belonged in a museum. "Go on," she said, jutting her chin out toward the door. "See if it works."

I felt a little like Alice in Wonderland as I fitted the bizarre old key to the lock. It turned easily with a bit of a squeak, and the sturdy door opened beneath my hand.

I guess I'd been expecting more "Downton Abbey" or *Wuthering Heights* beyond the door, with decaying red drapes, scarlet carpet that would swallow my flats and feet up to my ankles, and a canopied bed with far too many pillows that Jane Austen might have thought looked comfy. But I was very wrong.

Beyond the door was a beautiful little room, the walls painted a bright turquoise blue, the bed plain and modern with a purple duvet cover and two plump blue pillows that were different—but not jarring—from the wall's color, set at angles on top of the coverlet. There was a nice old wardrobe, and a cushy-looking blue chair that seemed so comfortable that I immediately walked over to it and sat down. On the little mahogany table beside the chair was a stack of old hardcover books, and an empty mug for tea with an unopened box of organic earl grey beside it.

"How…" I began, picking up the light box of tea and turning it over and over in my hands, the plastic wrap crinkling beneath my fingers. Gwen stood in the doorway, my suitcase at her feet and a knowing smirk on her face as she crossed her arms.

"I told Kane some things you like. You know, that you love turquoise walls and earl grey…little stuff like that. She'd been asking about you. That's the thing about Kane," she said then, waving to the wall. "She's very…thoughtful."

"Thoughtful," I repeated quietly, staring down at the tea in my hands. I set the box on the table and sniffed a little, looking up at the cool blue warmth of

35

the walls. I closed my eyes and leaned back in my chair. It was strange. I was...content.

The odd thing was, I couldn't remember the last time I could have called myself anything even close to "content." I opened my eyes, glanced at Gwen, who was now grinning smugly in the doorway as she toed my heavy suitcase forward and shut the door behind her. She leaned against it, glancing around again. I followed her gaze, taking in the little mini-fridge, the microwave sitting next to it on a broad mahogany serving table. There was a mahogany bookshelf, too, three shelves filled with old paperbacks, two standing empty. The curtains on the windows were drawn and tied back with scarlet bows, the curtains themselves a cheerful red color that went along with the blue marvelously.

I felt right at home, I realized. I didn't question that feeling—I went with it, sighing in contentment as I folded my hands over my stomach, crossing my legs in a slow, leisurely gesture.

"I'll come get you in the morning—show you around, introduce you to the other employees and everyone else," promised Gwen, crossing the room and giving me a great, big hug. She nodded toward my bathroom. "There'll be toiletries in there for taking a bath or a shower, and I'm sure she's stocked the fridge and freezer if you're hungry after all those fries," she teased. "I told her you were a vegetarian," she added, before I could protest. "So you'll be set. I'll come get you tomorrow morning at...say eight?"

"Sounds fine," I said, sinking deeper into the chair, glancing up at her with a smile. "Gwen..." I said, after she'd crossed back to the door, as she put her hand on the doorknob. "Thanks for looking out for me," I told her. And then, even quieter, I added: "I think I'm going to like it here. Thank you for everything."

"I hope you do," said Gwen with a grin, mouth all lopsided. "But wait to say that until after you meet Kane." She shut the door softly behind her and I was alone.

Not many people in the world would care if their walls were painted turquoise or not. She'd done this to make me feel welcome. I stood up, walked to the bookshelves, glancing over titles. What an incredibly thoughtful woman.

No matter what Gwen said, I thought I would like Kane very much.

I had no idea *how* much.

🌹

I was ready, dressed and waiting at seven fifty the next morning. But as the minutes slid by, one by one, I began to get restless waiting for Gwen to come fetch me. I paced in front of my big oaken door. I felt a little like a caged animal. I loved my rooms, but I was very curious about the Sullivan Hotel itself. Now that it was daylight, I wanted to see what it *really* looked like.

Eight came and went, eight *thirty* came and went, and Gwen was still not here.

I'd tried calling her cell phone, and I'd sent her two texts, all of them unanswered. Finally, I couldn't stand it any longer—my curiosity was getting to be a bit too much. I sent her one last text stating that I was going to venture out and explore the place, and then I did just that. I went to my big door, I turned the knob, and I opened it.

The hallway was cooler than my actual room, I noticed, as I shut the door softly behind me. I'd dressed in a black knee-length skirt, a bright blue blouse, and a black cardigan over it, but even with the extra layer, I shivered as I leaned against the cool wood behind me.

In the daylight, the bright colors of the doorframes down the corridor stood out even more than they had last night. I laid my hand on my own doorframe—last night's poison green was now a pleasant meadow color in the natural daylight. Gwen had informed me that Kane had put me in the green room because Gwen was in the pink room, right next door. Her pink doorframe was the shade of pink that they use for breast cancer awareness pins. I thought I heard a noise from within the room, but when I stepped up to the pink-bordered door and knocked on it, waiting, there was no answer. No one home. Gwen must have started out early, gotten caught up in her duties or something. I was sure she'd find me, or I'd find her eventually.

I set off down the hallway, my stomach rumbling. On the drive up, Gwen had told me that the employees of Sullivan Hotel could get anything we wanted to eat at pretty much any time from the kitchens, and from the cook there—a nice woman Gwen had told me was named Fiona. There was also breakfast, lunch and dinner served at regular times, though as I tried to remember those times, they escaped me. Maybe I could find my way downstairs and find the kitchens, get a bite to eat, and perhaps Gwen would be down there already.

I went down the corridor in the opposite direction from the one we'd come from last night. I don't know why. I wanted to see everything, wanted to take all of the architecture in, but mostly I just wanted to stare at the paintings on the walls, and one down the corridor to the right had caught my eye.

From what I'd gathered last night, Kane Sullivan was a great collector of art, and as I perused the pieces hung on the wall between the rooms' doors, I knew it to be true. There were great paintings here, paintings that made my heart flutter, that took my breath away. I couldn't imagine how much money she'd spent on the pieces of art on this stretch of hallway alone, let alone all of the stretches of hallway and rooms this sprawling mansion of a hotel seemed to have. As I continued walking down the hall, studying each painting in turn, the different styles swirling before my eye in a mixture of paint, artistic passion and the triumph of beauty, my heart began to stir in a way that it hadn't for a very long time.

Art's always been my driving passion, though I admit it's never paid my bills. Or, at least, that's what everyone told me would happen when I declared my major of art history in college. I suppose it shouldn't touch me now, that sad declaration that my passion would never make me a living, not all these years later, but that stigma's stuck, and I suppose it became a bit of a self-fulfilling prophesy. I went to school for something that made me happy, and it's never paid *any* of my bills, it's true. But it didn't matter to me. It made me *happy*. It still does.

That's the thing—art *was* my happiness. Besides Anna. And I stopped going to art galleries, openings, museums, after Anna died. I just didn't see any point in it anymore. What was beautiful in the world, if she wasn't there to share it with me? But I wondered, now, as I stopped in front of a particularly beautiful painting—a gorgeous landscape that looked American, perhaps 1920s, full of green, rolling hills and a few distant cows—if I shouldn't have stopped partaking in what made me happy. Maybe it would have helped me through her death, helped see me out to the other side if I had gone to museums, if I'd looked at beautiful art.

I didn't pay attention to steps or turns or which direction I was going as I walked along. I simply followed the art. Though there was a sea of beauty and the paintings began to blur in front of my eyes, several pieces still managed to stand out to me: one of a girl with a rabbit in her arms, done by the same artist who did portraits of Marie Antoinette a very long time ago. This girl's dress was so blue that it made my eyes ache, her expression playful and insolent, like she was hiding something besides the rump of the rabbit in her hands. There was a painting of four horses, their heads reared back in fear or triumph, it was difficult to tell. If you stepped far enough back, they looked savage and joyful. If you stepped closer, they looked terrified. Here was a painting of several young children, clustered around their mother's skirts while a father, his arm in a bandage, held her hand lovingly. Here a nude of a woman, her body resplendent as she threw her head back, her arms spread, storm clouds growing overhead like an omen.

It was then that I reached the staircase.

I hadn't realized that I had been following a sound for the past few moments, not until then. But there they were, two murmuring voices just out of reach enough for me to be unable to make out what it was they saying, but even though the words were muffled and unrecognizable, I still knew Gwen was one of the speakers, easily. She has this really bright voice that you could probably hear through six feet of concrete. It's the kind of voice that makes you smile.

The voices were down one simple flight of steps, and as I stared down the steep stairs, I recognized the red and black checkerboard of the first floor. I hadn't counted how many times I'd gone down staircases, but I must have gone down all of them. So *this* was the staircase from last night, next to the front desk. The Widowmaker. It must be. I'd never seen a steeper set of stairs. From up above, they looked simply like the rungs of a ladder in a barn—so steep and so tall and almost impossible to even think of taking.

It's not that I don't like heights—I'm pretty okay with them. But these stairs were something else. I wasn't taking these steps—I'd have to circle back somehow and find the other spiral staircase down to the first floor.

As I turned, I caught the first floor out of the corner of my eye. Because of the cathedral ceilings of that first floor, it seemed much farther away then I'd thought it was.

It was then that something strange happened.

The ground seemed to spin under me for a moment, bucking and heaving like I was trying to walk on waves of carpeting, not good, firm floor. Or did it really? Was it just a trick of the eye? Either way, I took a step backward as a shadow fell in front of me, but there was no floor beneath that foot stepping backward, then, and I was *tumbling* backwards, shock cold enough to burn me flooding through my body as, impossibly, I began to fall backwards down the stairs.

A hand caught my arm. I hung suspended over the abyss of the air, my back to the emptiness, and in one smooth motion, I was pulled back.

Saved.

The hand was cold, and the body I brushed against as I was hauled out of the air felt as if the person had stepped out of a prolonged trip through a walk-in freezer. I looked up at the face of the woman who had saved me, and when I breathed out, I will never forget it: my breath hung suspended in the air between us like a ghost.

She was taller than me by about a head, and I had to lean back to gaze into her eyes. They were violently blue, a blue that opened me up like a key and lock as she looked down at me, her eyes sharp and dark as her jaw worked, her full lips in a downward curve that my own eyes couldn't help but follow. She wore a ponytail, the cascades of her silken white-blonde hair gathered tightly at the back of her head and flowing over her right shoulder like frozen water falling. She wore a man's suit, I realized, complete with a navy blue tie smartly pulled snug against her creamy neck. She looked pale and felt so cold as her strong hand gripped my wrist, but it was gentle, too. As if she knew her own strength.

I saw all of this in an instant, my eyes following the lines and curves of her like I'd trace my gaze over an extremely fine painting. And, like an extremely fine painting, she began to make my heart beat faster. That was odd. I was never much attracted to random women, even before I dated Anna, even before Anna...well.

But this wasn't just my heart beating faster, my blood moving quicker through me. This was something else. A weightlessness, like being suspended in the air over the staircase again, the coolness of her palm against my skin a gravity that I seemed to suddenly spin around. When she gazed down into my eyes, she held me there as firmly as if her hands were snug against the small of my back, pressing me to her cool, lean body that wore the suit with such dignity and grace that I couldn't imagine her in anything else.

I was spellbound.

She said not a word, but her fingers left my wrist, grazing a little of the skin of my bare forearm for a heartbeat before her hand fell to her side. I shivered, holding my hand to my heart, then, as if I'd been bitten. We stood like that for a moment, two, the woman's eyes never leaving mine as her chin lifted, as her jaw worked again, her full lips parting...

"Are you all right?" I shivered again. Her voice was dark, deep and throaty, as cool as her skin, as gentle as the touch of her fingertips along my arm. But as I gazed up at her, as I tried to calm my breathing, my heart, we blinked, she and I, together.

I knew, then.

I'd heard that voice before.

I'd seen this *face* before.

"Have we...met?" I stammered, eyes narrowed as I gazed up at her in wonder. We couldn't have. She shook her head and put it to the side as she looked down at me, as if I was a particularly difficult puzzle that needed solving. I would have remembered her, the curve of her jaw and lips, the dazzling blue of her eyes. I could never have forgotten her if I'd only seen her once. It would have been impossible.

I took a gulp of air and took a step back again, unthinking, and her hand was there, then, at my wrist again as she smoothly pulled me forward, toward her.

"The stairs," she said softly, apologetically. I'd taken a step closer to her this time, and there was hardly any space between us, even as I realized that my hand was at her waist, steadying myself against her. I took a step to the side, quickly then, my cheeks burning.

"I'm sorry," I managed, swallowing. "And...thank you..." Her head was still to the side, but this time, her lips twitched as if she was trying to suppress a smile.

"I've been meaning to remodel these steps. Not everyone knows how steep they truly are," she said, and her lips did turn up into a smile, then, causing a flutter under my skin, inside my ribs. I took a great gulp of air as she held out her cool fingers to me, palm up.

"I am Kane Sullivan," she said easily, her tongue smoothing over the syllables as the smile vanished from her face. "You must be Rose Clyde," she said gently, the thrill of her voice, the deepness of it, the darkness of it, saying my name, the way her lips formed the words...I nodded my head up and down woodenly, and I placed my hand in hers. Her fingers were *so cold*, as she shook my hand like a delicate thing, letting her palm slide regretfully over mine as she dropped my hand with a fluid grace I had to watch but still couldn't fully understand.

I was acting like an idiot. I'd seen beautiful women before. But Kane wasn't beautiful. Not in that sense. She was...compelling. Her face, her gaze, her eyes, an impossibility of attraction. I felt as I watched her that buildings, trees, people would turn as she walked past them, unseeing things still, somehow, gazing at her.

I knew her, then.

The painting. The woman in the painting from last night, with the big, black cat, lounging and regal and triumphant and unspeakably bewitching. The naked woman, I realized, as my face began to redden, warming beneath her cool, silent gaze. She was the woman from the painting. But as I realized that, as we silently watched one another, I that this would have been impossible. It had been awhile since college, it was true, but I could still tell when a painting was a few hundred years old.

The woman in the painting could not possibly have been Kane Sullivan. And yet, it couldn't possibly have been anyone else.

"I...I'm sorry," I spluttered, realizing—again—how much of an idiot I must look to this incredibly attractive creature. Her lips twitched upward again, and her mouth stretched into a true smile this time, the warmth of it making the air around her seem less frozen.

"You're fine. It's not everyday that someone completely uproots their life and charts a course for places unknown," she said, turning on her heel and inclining her heard toward me. As she turned, I caught the scent of her. Jasmine, vanilla...spice. An intoxicating, cool scent that was warm at the same time. Unmistakable and deeply remarkable. Just like her. I stared up at her with wide eyes as she gestured gracefully with her arm for us to walk together, like she was a gentleman from the past century. True, she was wearing a sharp man's suit (that I was trying desperately not to stare at or trace the curves of it with my eyes—and failing), but there was something incredibly old-fashioned about her. I kept thinking about that at that first meeting. Like she was from a different era, not the one of smart phones and the Internet and fast food french fries. No. The kind of era that had horse-drawn carriages, corsets and bustles and houses that contained parlors. We began to walk down the corridor together, in the opposite direction I had come, me sneaking surreptitious glances at her, her staring straight ahead.

The spell of the moment was broken, but a new spell was beginning to create itself, weaving around the two of us as we walked along the corridor. As she spoke, I stared half up at her, half down the hall stretching out in front of us. All of my actual attention, though, was on this woman.

Every bit of it. She was just like that, so…compelling. She was a gravity that pulled me in, hook, line and sinker. I didn't know then how much of a gravity she had yet to become to me.

"I'm sorry that Gwendolyn could not meet you at the appointed time this morning to show you around and introduce you to everyone as she'd promised. She told me that had been her plan…but we had a pipe break in the kitchens," said Kane, every word apologetic as she glanced sidelong at me. "I was actually on my way to fetch you in her place, but…I passed the 'Widowmaker' on my way. And there you were."

The Widowmaker. Oh…those terrible stairs that had almost cost me my life. The name finally made sense.

"Thank you so much for hiring me," I managed, then, realizing that I'd not actually thanked her for the job and the room and the board and the change of life I hadn't known how much I needed. "I couldn't believe you hired me sight unseen," I confessed as we rounded a corner. The plush carpet beneath us caused our footsteps to be as hushed as a whisper as we walked side by side companionably. When had the floor changed underfoot from wood to carpeting? I wasn't paying attention to much of anything but her.

"But of course!" said Kane, and I glanced at her. She was smiling again, eyes on the floor in front of her, arms carefully folded behind her, head slightly to the side as if she was still trying to solve an interesting problem. I was beginning to wonder if *I* was that interesting problem. "Gwen's only been with me for a short while, but I trust her. She recommended you wholeheartedly, and how could I refuse such a sincere recommendation for employment? And, honestly, when she'd told me your circumstances..." She trailed off, and I saw her glance at me out of the corner of her eye.

My stomach began to roil in me. Circumstances? What exactly had Gwen told my new boss?

"She said that...you'd had had a family tragedy," said Kane smoothly, brows up. She appeared to notice my concern. "And that you needed a change of scenery."

Family tragedy. Yes, that perfectly described what had happened. Anna had been my only family. I sighed and rubbed at my eyes, staring down at my palm that now had a smudge of mascara in it. I'd forgotten I was wearing makeup. I didn't usually. But I'd wanted to make a good impression...and now I probably looked like a frazzled fright. Great. But Kane didn't make any mention of it at all, only smiled softly at me and pulled a handkerchief, of all things, out of her suit jacket's breast pocket. I felt like I'd stepped back in time as I took the cloth handkerchief from her, and dabbed beneath my eyes. The corner of the cloth came away a little black, and I sighed, staring down at the square of cream in my hands that I'd now effectively stained forever.

"You keep it," said Kane, voice soft, as I turned the cloth over and over again in my palms, staring down at the perfectly monogrammed fancy red "S" in the corner. I traced my finger along its delicate scarlet curve. "My mother taught me," she said, mouth forming a grimace now, "to always have a handkerchief handy. Just in case."

"You'd think I would have learned that important lesson," I realized I'd blurted out before I could stop myself. "These past few months have been especially hard for me. Which is why I'm extra grateful for the change of scenery in coming here...to the Sullivan Hotel," I told her, as we approached a heavily ornamented oaken door. The thing was massive, at least twice as tall as I was, and we stopped outside of it, then. I heard voices from within. Women's voices. Laughter.

Music.

Kane smiled at me again, and it was so strange when she did so. The woman in the painting...had she been smiling? I couldn't remember if she was or not, but regardless, I felt as if I'd seen Kane smile before. It was such a rich, delicious thing to watch this woman smile. She was very certain about her smiles, and I got the feeling—very much so, in fact—that she didn't often do it, lips curling up at the corners, face brightening like a star. Somehow, I felt that when she smiled, it was a rare and precious thing.

And now here she was. Smiling at *me*.

What was wrong with me? There was a distant, strange feeling, as if I was doing something wrong. I knew where that feeling was coming from. Anna. I'd loved her so much, and now here my stomach was turning warm, my heart beating faster, because this incredible woman was smiling at me. But there was something else even beyond that, in this strange feeling. Something—well. Stranger.

It was unnerving because I felt as if I'd seen her before. As if I'd seen her smile at me, reach out her hand to me. As if she'd touched me before. There was something familiar about the soft coolness of her skin, and it could not *possibly* be familiar. But it was, at the same time.

As we stood quietly in the corridor, as the sound of muffled voices, of velvety laughter, played out in the room beyond, we stood together. The air between us was cool, scented with jasmine and spice. It was intoxicating, and again for the second time that day, I felt light headed.

I felt *so strange*.

"I wanted to introduce you to the others here at the Sullivan Hotel," said Kane then, inclining her head back toward the massive oaken door behind her. The wide doorframe around the impressive doors was carved with twining maple leaves, violets, and—upon closer inspection—little cherubim faces, though they did not look at all angelic. Their wings curved behind them in such a way that it looked almost as if they had devil horns. Paired with their demonic smirks, they were more than a little unnerving. I shivered.

Kane turned back to me. "These are my…relatives," she said then mysteriously, as she smiled at me again. "They all live here at the Sullivan Hotel with me, and most of the employees simply treat them as if they were guests, so you'll probably interact with them quite a bit. They are very important to me," she said strangely, brows up. I wiped my sweaty palms against my skirted thighs, clearing my throat nervously as she placed her long, graceful fingers on the elaborately scrolled silver doorknob.

The door opened.

"You take forever—we thought you'd be back a half hour ago!" said the woman at the door petulantly, stomping her pink high-heeled toe a little. She had short curly blonde hair, and a doll's downward curving painted red mouth, perfectly makeupped face making her appear model-like. She was frowning as she gazed at Kane, but then she saw me and grinned widely. "The new girl!" she announced then, flinging the door wide open.

Kane ushered me into the dimly lit room. Though it was morning, and windows along the corridor had proclaimed it a remarkably sunny, pretty day outdoors, there were no windows in this room, making it seem smaller and darker within than it really was. It took me a moment for my eyes to adjust to the darker interior, and it was then that I realized how many women were here, lounging on couches or plush chairs, or standing together in a little group. Eight women, I realized.

"Sullivans," said Kane, sweeping her arm to include the room and all of its shadowed occupants. "Meet Rose Clyde, our newest employee here at the hotel. And Rose? Meet the Sullivans."

There was something strange that I couldn't quite work out as my eyes adjusted even further to the dimly lit room, and I was able to fully take in the women. I finally recognized the strangeness as I looked at them.

None of the women looked similar.

But they were...the Sullivans? Were they related? But how could they be?

The petulant blonde woman who'd opened the door to us grinned widely at me and held out her perfectly pink-nailed hand. "I'm Dolly," she cooed, pumping my hand up and down energetically. "We're so pleased to have you here! You're going to *love* it in Eternal Cove, I promise—"

"Try not to eat her up in one gulp, Doll," murmured one of the women lounging on the corner plush couch. Though her words were soft and low, they carried with authority across the room to us. She had long, straight black hair and as I glanced in her direction, I felt myself paling. I'd never seen a more beautiful, cat-like woman filling out the curves of a prettier black dress. The dress looked a little retro, like it was from the fifties with all its pleats and ruffles, and the dress clung to every curve of her, as if it had been dripped over her skin to form the fabric. A thick necklace of pearls hung in drapes around her neck as she curled her too-red lips upward. She was very pale, I realized, as I watched her stand, her tall heels clicking over the red and black checkerboard floor toward us in measured, calculating steps, her body moving in the confidant, almost lazy strides of a big cat. Her smile didn't quite reach her eyes.

She held out her hand to me, too, and when I took hers and shook it, her fingernails seemed to prick my palms.

"I'm Mags," she told me then, leaning forward a

little, eyebrows arching towards Kane as she dropped my hand like it was a bit of trash. "And no offense, sugar," she said, wiping her palm on her hip as I blushed. She wasn't looking at me as she spoke—she was staring at Kane. "But this little morsel isn't going to last two minutes here." Her lips were up and over her teeth, now, as if she was sneering...but it was more of a snarl.

I was so surprised by this hostile gesture that I took a step backwards. But then Kane's hand was at the small of my back, and I was so equally surprised by her protectiveness, that I stood still, instead. Kane took a step closer to Mags, her fingers curling around my waist as she leaned forward. The air between the two women seemed to snap, crackling with the energy between their locked eyes.

The room fell silent.

"Manners, Mags," is what Kane whispered, then. It was such a soft tone of voice that I had to strain to hear it, but the syllables seemed to reverberate in the floor beneath my flats.

Mags stared from me to Kane back to me again, and then she laughed. She tilted back her head and laughed like she'd just heard the most ridiculous joke. It was a cruel collection of cackles. She turned and clicked back over to the couch. It was almost a flounce.

I didn't understand the exchange, really. But it was quite obvious, then, that Mags and Kane didn't exactly see eye to eye.

I'd last here much more than a minute, thanks *ever* so much, I told myself, bristling. I'd last as long as I *wanted* to here. And why *wouldn't* I last? All Gwen had told me about this place sounded like wonderful things, and if there were minuses to the job, she would have said something to me about them. I knew that. But as I watched Mags prowl back to the couch, her hips swaying back and forth as if it was their job to be suggestive, I swallowed. She moved like a predator.

"Don't listen to Mags," said the woman closest to me, then. Though it was only about nine o'clock in the morning, she was holding an empty martini glass in two graceful black fingers. She had one brow up, her curly, short black hair sweeping over her eyes like she'd styled it to be reminiscent of Elvis. "She's in a permanent bad mood," said the woman, her warm, rich voice sweeping over me. She grinned at me with her full lips as if we shared a secret. "I think you'll fit in quite well here. My name is Victoria."

"Hello, Victoria," I told her, as monotone as if I was a robot repeating words. Dolly pranced up to me again, as if sensing how overwhelmed I was, her high heels clicking on the impressive black and red floor as she snatched up my hand and squeezed it.

"Play a round of gin rummy with me?" she said then, plaintive words seemingly curled up at the end, not as if she was asking me, but rather demanding that I do it. I didn't mind as I gazed over my shoulder at Kane who shrugged and smiled a little, gesturing with her hand to the rickety card table set up in the corner with the worn deck of cards spread out at it. They were spread out on a doily that did little to mask how beat up the table was—which seemed deeply incongruous with the grandeur of the rest of the furniture in the room. But Dolly dragged me over and I sat down woodenly at the table, trying to take in all of the women in the room, the room itself with all of its dark, shadowed corners, and the fact that all of these women were gathered here rather than in a dining hall for breakfast

53

or in the kitchens, or...

"I found our Rose by the Widowmaker. If I hadn't caught her, she would have fallen down the steps," said Kane then, voice low as she strode with purpose toward the far mantel and fireplace. A fireplace, I might add, that was wide enough to drive a car through. The carved marble mantle again had the maple leaves, the violets...and those frightening cherubim faces that seemed to grimace at me as I turned to watch Kane move. Kane opened up an ornate little wooden box that was set on that mantle and—much to my surprise—took out a pack of cigarettes. She tapped one out with practiced ease, and lit it with a strange little contraption that looked like it was a curvaceous woman made out of metal. An antique lighter, I realized.

"Fallen!" snorted Mags, crossing her legs and twitching her toes up and down so that her high heel moved with rhythm. "We wouldn't want that."

That wasn't even a thinly veiled threat—it was a clumsy overture of hatred. I stared at this woman I'd just met, this woman who believed—for whatever strange reason—that I'd last five minutes in this hotel, in this job.

My incredibly articulate thought of "what the hell?" was brought up short as I swallowed, folding my hands in my lap. I was not going to let this strange woman get to me.

Dolly glanced up at me, but only for half a heartbeat, and surreptitiously, as if she didn't want me noticing she'd glanced my way. She shuffled the cards expertly, her pink nails flashing as she snorted. "You're such a bitch, Mags," she said, flipping the cards almost in the air as she rearranged the cards to chance again and again. I watched her hands, my heartbeat racing, watched the cards flash like silver fish between us.

Kane took a long pull on the cigarette, like a movie star from the forties, savoring the inhalation as deeply as a woman from the forties would—before the knowledge that the smoke could do any harm whatsoever to you had been found out. She blew the smoke out slowly and stalked over to us—fully ignoring Mags. Kane moved with purpose, almost going slowly, each foot finding its perfect spot to step, so that she moved like a predator, too, I realized.

Once Kane was beside us, she leaned against the wall, taking another pull on the cigarette as she regarded me with those violently blue eyes of hers. "Do you mind if I smoke?" she asked me softly, her head to the side in that curious way, staring at me intently, waiting for me to answer. I realized I'd been staring at the cigarette.

"No...not at all," I murmured as Dolly chuckled behind her hand, shuffling through the cards one last time before leaving the stack of them perfect and neat on the wooden table in front of her.

She dealt the ten cards not even looking at the slick pieces of paper in her fingers. I only noticed this out of the corner of my eye, because I was really watching Kane. Watching as smoke wreathed her head like a halo, almost obscuring those too-blue eyes as she pulled again and again on the cigarette.

But Kane was watching *me*. I took the cards as Kane flicked the cigarette, the ash on the ends sailing in the air as light as breath. My fingers were numb with cold as I touched the cards, hyper-aware of how cool the air was in the space between Kane's body and mine, hyper-aware of her eyes on me.

Dolly's smile was wide, as if we were sharing a joke as her fingers curled around her own cards.

We played the game.

I'm not very good at card games. Not that it mattered. I wasn't paying attention to the game, and I wasn't paying attention to Dolly. She made occasional jokes, but—for the most part—we played it in silence. And Kane watched. The air around the woman may have been cold, but the heat of her gaze seemed to burn a line into my skin, tracing my curves, my hands, my form and face. I shivered beneath that intense gaze, and occasionally, I would lift my eyes to her. She looked away each time, slowly, carefully, as if it was imperative that we not lock eyes or exchange glances. She smoked through several cigarettes, always expertly lighting the next one from the stub in her long fingers, and rich blue smoke continued to rise around her face like she was an angel, and the clouds of heaven had parted so she could look down through them to me.

What was happening? I flipped cards and looked at numbers and spades and clubs and diamonds...and hearts. And my own heart beat a little faster, and my own face was warmed and red, and as I played the game with Dolly, it was the strangest thing...it was familiar. Dolly was familiar, yes, with her lilting, high-pitched laugh and her soft blonde ringlets. But this, too, was all familiar. The snipes and occasional jabs from Mags, the laughter and low, murmured conversation from the other women. The room with its tall walls of stained, antique wood, the red and black checkerboard floor, the antique furniture that gave off that scent that antiques do: a little musty, and a little like memories.

But the most familiar thing of all was Kane's

presence, beside me. Watching me. Making me shiver beneath her gaze.

Somehow, impossibly, Dolly was gathering the cards from beneath our hands, and declaring "I won again!" The cards flashed in her palms as she shuffled, crossing her legs and leaning back in her chair as she regarded me with a bemused quirk of her lips. "We can stop, now, Rose. I've beaten you too many times. Thanks for playing with me."

My head was heavy, my eyes heavy-lidded as if I'd gone days without sleep, the smoke swirling about my face mingling with the wood smoke from the fireplace. Though a fire roared in the wide grate, the warmth didn't reach us here, and my skin crawled with goosebumps. I could feel gazes on me, watching me, as if curious, but just as many of the women hadn't given me the time of day or seemed to notice me in any way.

That was the strange thing. If I was an employee of this hotel, what was I doing hanging out with the owners?

And *were* there owners, or was it just Kane? And why did it feel like I'd done this before, known her before...as if these actions, this playing cards with Dolly while Kane smoked and watched, her eyes raking over my form, was as familiar as if I'd slipped on a well-worn glove?

I remember this line from a book my mother read me when I was a kid. I'm sure everyone's read it: *Alice in Wonderland*. I didn't particularly like it—it was too confusing to me when I was eight, and I've never given it a chance since. But there was this one line that's always stuck with me, that I've always remembered and thought about. And it was worth using now:

Curiouser and curiouser.

As if playing gin rummy before a roaring fire wasn't strange enough, I then heard the plucked strings of a violin as a woman tuned it behind us. I felt as if I'd fallen backwards in time about a century as a woman with burnished brown hair, close-cropped to her skull, and wearing a suit just like Kane's, drew a bow across the violin's strings, eliciting an eerie, almost human sound of music.

And then she began to play.

She was very good. I didn't recognize the melody, but I almost did, an old classical piece that Dolly began to tap her toe to as she placed the stacked and shuffled cards in front of her on the table, turning to listen to this music player. Is this what they did all day, I wondered, as I glanced around the room again. There was no television, no laptops, no smart phones that I could see, and that's what I think was the strangest thing of all.

Cards and violin music and talking and laughter. It really *was* like a moment from the past as the cigarette smoke twirled in loops and swirls across the ceiling. As if we'd all stepped backward into a corridor of time, into an intimate hall somewhere in Europe where women dressed like men laughed and kissed each other, drawing velvet-clad ladies onto their laps to wrap their arms around their soft forms.

Maybe it was wrong to assume that all of the women in this room were lesbians, but they very much seemed that way to me. Maybe the name "Sullivan" was code for something, because hadn't Kane introduced everyone here to me as a Sullivan? I'd come across a lot of nicknames for "lesbian" in my long and illustrious career as one (hah! Far from illustrious), but

I'd never heard "Sullivan." But how could they all be related...?

My brain was twisting inward on itself, and I felt disoriented, discombobulated...weird. As the violin music rose into the air, wrapping itself around us as tightly as the smoke, Mags began to move toward me through the gray air, smile twisting on her face as she held out her sharp-nailed hand to me.

"Would you like to dance?" she asked, and I shuddered, because I thought she was making a joke at my expense as I stared up at her. There was something dangerous in those eyes.

She looked hungry.

I shook my head. "I'm sorry, I don't dance," is what I told her as the women quieted, turning to the both of us. Probably to see how Mags was going to slice me to pieces with words. But I held my gaze with the woman whose sardonic smile turned into a frown as she glanced from me to Kane again, one brow rising in a slash of black across her too-pale face.

"She doesn't dance," she all but cooed as she sashayed past Kane, shaking her head, her hands on her hips. Kane regarded her calmly, coolly, as Mags went past. "Funny," hissed Mags, drawing out the word to imply that it was, actually, not funny at all. "But Kane doesn't dance either. What stuff you both have in common! Two of a kind!"

"I...I'm sorry," I managed, stumbling to my feet. I was light-headed, the floor swirling beneath me as quickly as it had by the Widowmaker staircase. "I have to go..." I said. The smoke, the coolness, the strange feelings...it was too much. I moved past Dolly, past Mags, past all the other women, but as I passed Mags, her hand snaked out and she took my wrist. Her

59

fingers were so cold that it seemed—for half a heartbeat—that they'd burned my skin.

"Don't forget to watch your step," she chuckled, low and throaty, in my ear before releasing my wrist from her grip. I moved past her, not looking back until I'd reached the door, my fingers curling around the silver scrollwork of the doorknob. Only then did I turn, look back into the room.

Everyone else had returned to their individual pastimes. Only Kane watched me, the brilliance of her blue eyes cutting through the smoke and the darkness. I breathed out, my breath catching in my lungs, and then the doorknob was turned, and I was out into the corridor, the room closed behind me.

I leaned against the door for a long moment, taking in deep breaths of fresh air. Kane's scent seemed to cling to the strands of my hair that were curling around my neck and over my shoulders, now. Warm spice and vanilla.

I stayed for a long moment with my hand on the doorknob, as if I was compelled to return, as if I'd do anything to be within Kane's gaze again. I wrenched my hand from the knob and took two steps away from the door.

Out of the floor-length windows, the sun touched against the earth, a bright explosion of reds, oranges and golds.

Sunset?

How was that possible? How long had I been in that room?

Behind the oaken door, laughter as brittle as breaking glass echoed.

And then the low tones of Kane's voice. The laughter was silenced as I turned and walked back along the hallway, shivering.

Somehow, impossibly, I found the way back to my rooms and my bathrobe and the boxed food in the freezer that went into the microwave and then into my stomach. I don't remember what I ate or how I made it or how I found the utensils to eat it with. I was in a haze. I wanted to talk to Gwen, *needed* to talk to her, but she wasn't in her rooms.

I fell asleep with my feet on the little antique ottoman, and my body curled up on the bright blue chair, the handkerchief Kane had given me clutched in one hand.

And I dreamed.

I couldn't stop thinking about Kane, which is how I explained the dream, afterward. She was the last thought that I'd had before falling asleep, so of course she would be the thing I dreamed of. Of course. But that calm explanation didn't exactly reach me in that moment as I realized I was dreaming, as I opened my dreaming eyes, and she was standing in front of me.

Kane Sullivan.

Her white-blonde hair almost glowed beneath the moonlight, luminous and bright. We were out standing on a broken sidewalk, bits of concrete pressing through the thin bottom of my flats against the skin of my feet as I shifted, leaning toward her. Maybe we were in my old town, maybe we were in Eternal Cove, though it was hard for me to say, since I'd not seen Eternal Cove hardly at all, just that first time that Gwen drove me through it on the way to the Sullivan Hotel.

Either way, no matter where we were *exactly*, we

now stood on a sidewalk in front of an old, gothic church. The steeple loomed overhead, long and thin and sharp, like a needle. I was wearing my favorite red jacket, the one with the soft pockets and the satin lining. She was wearing her men's suit, a single white rose at a hole in the lapel, its petals soft and almost glowing, too, in the darkness of the night. The wind was soft and cool as it played with her hair, moving it this way and that as she stood in front of me, her hands deep in her suit jacket pockets. Her eyes were that same violent blue, the blue so dark and deep and bright, all at the same time, that when she stared into me, it seemed—as cheesy as it sounds—that she was seeing to the depths of my soul and back again.

Something stirred in my belly as our gazes locked, as we stood about a foot apart, the coolness of her skin washing over mine, even though there were those twelve short inches between us, and she was not, in fact, actually touching me. Everything about her was a gravity, I realized, as she held out her hand to me. I couldn't *not* place my fingers within her palm, I couldn't *not* step forward as she pulled me gently, tugging my arm so that I glided forward effortlessly, my curves resting along hers, our bodies against one another like they were made to be this way, complementing and whole.

She stared down into my eyes, tilting back my chin with one long finger, the coolness of her skin making me shiver, but this shiver, I now knew, was one of delight. As she stared down at me, the depth of her eyes growing deeper, bluer, truer, I inhaled that scent of her, the coolness of her that was so opposite to the spice of her, inhaling deeply as her lips hovered above mine, and I wanted—more than anything else that I've ever wanted—to stretch up on my tiptoes and kiss her.

But I did not kiss her, and she did not kiss me. She paused in her downward descent toward me, she paused as her exquisite, graceful neck angled her face gently down toward mine, the light from the moon dangling overhead like a lantern painting her face with sharp angles and lovely valleys of light.

She paused and she stopped, and she did not kiss me, and though I wanted—desperately—more than anything to kiss her, I did not. I don't know why I stopped myself. I suppose I knew that this wasn't the right time and place, this dream, this fantasy.

I wanted the real thing.

I woke up.

I sighed and rubbed at my face in the darkness, my heart beating too quickly in me to want to try and fall back asleep, to even attempt such a thing. The handkerchief pressed the scarlet "S" against my palm, and I turned it over in my hand with a frown.

I got up and checked my wristwatch that I'd placed on the little oaken bedside table. I peered down at the tiny face in the half-light coming in through the window of the streetlamps above the little parking lot outside and sighed. Four o'clock in the morning. Great. I was supposed to get up at seven, and that meant that if I didn't fall back asleep now, I...wouldn't. And tomorrow would be an extremely over-tired hell, the very first day of my actual employment here at the Sullivan Hotel.

But it couldn't be helped. I knew with utter surety that I wasn't getting back to sleep anytime soon.

I got up out of bed again, threw on my favorite red jacket over my pajama top and bottom (the very embarrassing fleece set of 'jammies, covered with gigantic cartoonish lips. Gwen had gotten it for me a few years ago as a joke, when absurd fleece pajamas were pretty popular. But her joke had misfired: I'd actually enjoyed them because they were *crazily* soft and warm. Who cared about gigantic cartoonish lips in the face of extreme softness and warmth?). I pulled on my old floppy brown hat with the earflaps and tugged on my worn gloves, and I slipped out of my room, the heavy metal key resting in my coat pocket against my thigh like a trusted, familiar weight.

    Everything was quiet, softly quiet, the perfect silent time of night that makes me…well. *Happy*. I don't know why. When I was a kid, I'd often wake up in the three o'clock hour, and I'd read until I fell back asleep, then often have dreams about whatever I'd been reading about (usually vampires, if you'd believe it). But when I was a teenager and I woke up in that strange three o'clock hour I'd grown to know, and almost love, I began a tradition that exists until this very day. I'd get up, get dressed…and I'd go for a walk.

    I used to walk down the streets of my old town at three o'clock in the morning without a care in the world. I know a lot of people think that walking at such an ungodly hour is pretty unsafe, but nothing ever happened to me, and I had a little can of pepper spray in my other coat pocket, just in case. And, true, tonight was very different from those long-ago walks. For one thing, I didn't know my way around this place that well yet, but I'd found my way back to my rooms from the second floor, and if I avoided the Widowmaker staircase (because pretty much forever I'd be avoiding the Widowmaker staircase), I'd be able to make it to the first floor and out into the cool night. It wasn't a very *good* plan, admittedly, but my head was still muddled from the amount of hours I'd spent in that room with those women.

It felt strange, muzzy, the memory of today. I wondered if it had even happened.

The only evidence I had that I did not, in fact, dream up Dolly and Mags and Kane staring at me deeply through the shadows, was the fact that my hair smelled lightly of cigarette smoke. Normally, the scent of smoke tickles my nose—it's dirty and dark, and I don't like it. But this smoke was different. Spicy, almost. Still cancer-causing, obviously, but also almost sweet and edgy. I *liked* it, despite everything in me telling me that I absolutely should not.

So it *had* really happened. I'd spent all day with these women, and I'd not needed to eat or drink, and time had seemed to speed up or…I don't know. I didn't have any other explanation other than that, that time—in fact—had actually moved faster than normal within that dark, mysterious room. It seemed that only an hour or two had passed while I sat at the table with Dolly, playing cards, Kane's eyes warm and cool against me at the same time. But then the sunset had burnished the sky with gold, and I'd woken up from something that had felt so much like a dream…and my entire day had seemingly been stolen from me.

Honestly, "stolen" isn't the right word. "Stolen" implies that something was taken away from you that you valued, and you're unhappy with the experience. My day hadn't been stolen. I didn't mind any bit of it, because I'd spent the entire day within Kane's gaze.

Yes, I suppose you could say I was beginning to have it very, very bad for that woman. Which was crazy, I know. I didn't even have evidence that she was a lesbian, though it seemed pretty obvious that she was. There was just a feeling...a knowing that she very much might be.

And also a feeling that I knew her, her gaze, her form a familiar thing to me. From where or when or how...I didn't know.

So many strange feelings, and I had no place to put them. I had half a mind to wake Gwen up and talk with her until we were supposed to go on shift, sort out all these muddled feelings and half memories over warm cups of tea, curled up together, knee to knee on the couch, but that would have been cruel to a friend who had gotten me this strange job in the first place. Gwen slept through the night, arguably *needed* her sleep (you know, like most normal people tend to do) and the few times I'd ever woken her up with a phone call at these sorts of hours, she was mumbly and practically incoherent anyway.

So I found the spiral staircase leading down, and I followed it. Down and down and down until the very first floor and the dimly lit corridor of art that made the red and black checkerboard floor seem to glow dimly from all of the little lamps over each painting illuminated. I dug my hands into my coat pockets—the wide, open corridor was very chilly—and I walked with my head down, my steps wide and quick, devouring the space between myself and the front door.

The click of my boots against the floor echoed around me as I followed the curving hallway until I was alongside the front desk and the steep steps of the Widowmaker staircase. I stared up at it with wide eyes. It seemed impossible to me that anyone would call it anything but a ladder. It was impossibly steep—no wonder I'd almost fallen down it. It was this ramshackle, steep staircase that seemed like it might wobble and fall to pieces if you'd so much as look at it funny. Could it even support the weight of a single person? It was so incongruous with how magnificent and well-kept everything else in this place seemed to be.

The wide, wooden front desk was empty, not surprisingly, and I slipped past it without a sound, turning the large front door's knob with cold fingers.

And then I was outside, beneath an unspeakable amount of stars, the chill of the out-of-doors so sudden and cold that it seemed to snatch my breath from me as I shut the massive front door behind me. I stood very still on the stone front porch, and I listened, my ears pricking for sound in the velvet darkness of a too-early hour. That's when I heard it: the unmistakable *shush* of the ocean tide.

Gwen had told me that the Sullivan Hotel was located on a cliff face, and I had no desire to tumble to my death like a heroine in an old classic British novel (or BBC remake). But the lights in the small parking lot, a parking lot that was much too small for such a big hotel, illuminated a quaint, hand-painted wooden sign that had an arrow pointing toward a gravel-lined path. The words "Beach Trail" were painted in a red, looping script, with a curving, beckoning arrow pointing onward. I took a breath and huffed it out, my exhale curling up like smoke into the air, as I made a split-second decision and crossed the expanse of parking lot beneath the fluorescent bulbs. I entered the path to the beach trail, promising myself that if it grew too steep or was a bit too treacherous, I'd turn back.

The crunch of the gravel beneath my boots was a comforting rhythm. When I walked past the hedge of shrubs lining the parking lot, down the trail itself, the *shush* of the ocean became louder, brighter. Clearer, somehow. My eyes were still adjusting to the dark, but now I could see the ocean, spreading out beneath me.

The trail down to the beach was a wide expanse that had probably been used for cars or maybe even carts, once upon a time. It was about ten feet wide and cut into the actual rock side of the cliff. It sloped very gradually and gracefully downward, toward the beach. The beach itself was very easy to see—I wondered what color the sand was in the daylight, because now in the monochrome of night, it looked like brilliant white. The scent of the salt in the air lifted my spirits, and I began to feel less tired as I watched the white-cap waves rush toward the shore as I made my way down the path. The waves broke on the seemingly-white sand, and frothed up energetically.

When I reached the bottom of the trail, my boots hit the beach. I staggered a little as I gained my balance on the sand (reminding myself that I wouldn't wear boots with heels when I came this way again), and set off across the expansive beach, toward the line where the ocean met the shore.

Now, the sound was almost deafening, the crash of the water hitting the earth. It was also comforting, soothing, at the exact same time that it was slightly unnerving. I think that unless you've grown up with it, the sea at night is always a little bit of a frightening thing. The fear comes from our old memories from when we were still cavemen gathered closely around the fire to keep the dark away. The sea is something that we *still* don't fully understand, and tales of sea monsters are *still* told around campfires. I stood very still, my heels sinking backward into the sand, thinking about the darkness of the water, the whiteness of it breaking against the shore, the millions of stars I could see overhead as I tilted my head up and back.

I felt so small, so insignificant beneath that beautiful brilliance of starlight. I thought about Anna, and I thought about Kane, and as I stared up at the stars, I didn't feel guilt for thinking about either of them. Usually, I felt so much pain when I thought about Anna. And I did feel pain as I thought on her, yes. But it wasn't the fresh pain that I almost always felt. It was dull and quieter, now, and I could take a breath when I thought of her.

And when I thought of Kane...there was a flutter in my heart.

Should I have even been thinking about Kane? Had it been long enough since Anna? Half a year had come and gone since the accident, and it felt like a lifetime, and it felt like only a moment had passed, all at the same time. There were so many "shoulds" and "should nots" that it made my stomach turn, but I did my best, as I felt so small beneath those stars, to simply concentrate on what I was feeling. I didn't understand all of it, it was true. But Kane made me feel something that I hadn't felt in so long.

There was *possibility* in Kane.

Okay, maybe she wasn't a lesbian. Maybe she wouldn't want me, even if she was one. Maybe she was already taken. There was so much unknown and uncertain about this woman, but that was all right. I didn't know, and as I stood beneath that glorious spread of stars, next to the seemingly unending ocean, there was just...possibility.

And for the first time in what seemed like forever...I felt something pricking inside of me, something growing and unfurling like a blossom opening in my heart.

It was hope.

It was at that moment that I saw the body in the water.

If my eyes hadn't become so adjusted to the monochrome of the night, I never would have seen that dark curve of shadow, out in the tossing white waves. But they had adjusted, and I could see as I looked out to the water, feeling a million things and feeling hope rise up in my chest, but it was all shattered in that instant. I blinked back the salt spray of the water, took a step forward, and my boot hit the incoming curl of the tide. What? What had I just seen? It must have been a fish. Or a shark. Or a dolphin. But as I trained my eyes on the incoming waves, I saw it again. Or I thought I saw it. A human form, waving arms above the water.

And then, so faint that it almost seemed not real, I heard the softest whisper of sound:

"Help me."

Another incoming wave, another glimpse of someone flailing pale arms above the water, and I didn't hesitate. I've always been a good swimmer. My mother insisted that I started taking lessons at my local pool by the age of three. I can swim in my sleep, but I'd never struggled out of a coat and boots on the water's edge in October in Maine. I threw back my coat and my boots farther up the shore so they wouldn't get taken by the tide, and then I stepped into the waves.

The shock of the cold took all of my breath as I staggered forward, half-jogging, half-tripping as I tried to find my way in deeper without getting knocked off my feet by the insistent waves. This close up, they seemed so much bigger, and they'd already seemed pretty big to me, the gigantic frothy things that kept churning milk-white foam up onto the shore. I tried to keep the figure in my sights as my feet were taken out from under me, and I set out with a strong breaststroke toward the person. But it was almost impossible to swim in this water. The salt stung my eyes as I tried to keep them open, as I tried to keep watching for this person, keep it in my sights, and the cold snatched my breath away.

The cold was *everywhere*, every last inch of me, inside and out. I'm the kind of person who can't even really stand a less-than-piping-hot shower, so as I tried to shoulder my way through the water, as I tried to just move through it and stay afloat, staying above and over those waves, I kept losing my breath. I felt the pounding of my heart, and everything shook, even as I tried to slice through the water toward the person.

The first frozen wave hit me full on in the face, and I took a great mouthful of water that somehow ended up a bit in my lungs, too. I surfaced, spluttering and coughing, trying to keep my breaths steady and long, even as my lungs hitched up, deeply unhappy at the freezing water I'd accidentally inhaled. I struggled to breathe, struggled to stay on the surface, struggled to stay alive as the frozen water pulled me down and under, pulled me farther out to sea.

I'd never been in waters like these before: black and icy and completely treacherous. All thoughts of the drowning person began to be covered up by the very real and present thought that maybe *I* was becoming a drowning person.

I spluttered upward again, my eyes wide open in the murky dark as I tried to find the surface after being pulled under again. How had I gotten out this far? I glanced backward toward shore, and the icy shock began to fill me as I realized exactly how far out I was. The cold of the water was making my muscles move slower, more sluggish. I could hardly breathe, and as I moved slower, like a wind-up toy that was slowly winding down, I felt fear begin to fill me up, much like the cold and the salt water. I tried to press through the water with my arms, pumping my legs with a sudden surge of adrenaline as I struggled against the waves.

Was this really how I was going to go? I kept thinking that, looping the thought around and around as my adrenaline became more pronounced, and I kicked harder against the frozen waves, as I sought to climb them with more strength. I took in a great lungful of air and suppressed the urge to cough it all back out, because of the bits of salt water still in my lungs. With the air in me, I rose a little higher in the water, the frozen water that was slowly numbing every part of me. I crested on the surface, and I glanced back toward shore again.

It was so much farther away.

That's when something bumped my leg.

I was too far out to even hope for it to be the sandy bottom of the ocean, but I still thought that desperately. Or maybe it was a rock, a rock I could stand on. But in the back of my mind, I knew absolutely that it was neither one of those things.

Whatever had hit me had been slightly pliable. Slightly soft. It had hit me much the same that the smack of meat against skin would feel like.

It was a living thing.

Panic set in. A shark. It was the only thing I could think of. I'd bumped into a shark. But a shark in

Maine in very, very cold October waters? But I had no sense, only fear, and fear makes us think very strange things. So no, it couldn't have been a shark, but I still thought it was one anyway. I kicked out violently to get away from the thing, kicked out and tried to turn my body, my body that the ocean was tearing farther and farther out to sea with frozen waters. I kicked out, trying to move even an inch back toward shore. But it was impossible.

And something bumped against my leg again.

I screamed. I got a mouthful of cold salt water for my efforts, and because of that, I lost the last of the air that had been making me a little buoyant, and I went underwater as I thrashed in my panic. I opened my eyes, trying desperately to see whatever it was that had bumped my leg.

There was a woman underwater.

The woman who had been drowning. I could see her black hair and her pale arms. She was wearing something that bared her arms. Pure instinct took over, and I grasped at one of those arms, trying to haul her up toward air, as much as I was trying to get myself there. I sunk down a little as I tried to pull her upward, and I felt her cold skin under my hand, slick and too cold for me to even hold, my numb fingers trying to maintain purchase of her. She was so heavy, impossibly heavy. She might already be dead. I didn't know. I just knew that I needed air, or I was going to die. But I couldn't leave her here.

I kicked with my legs, used my other arm to try and propel myself upwards, toward the roiling surface of the ocean with its white waves and its violent power.

I couldn't reach it. I couldn't haul her up, with my last reserves of strength, *and* reach the surface. It was one or the other. We were both going to die here. Or she could just die. And really, she might already be dead. She might. I might be doing all of this for a dead woman. I might be about to die for a dead woman.

But I couldn't let her go. I couldn't. Somewhere, within me, I found the last bits of strength. I scraped them together. I kicked with my legs and hauled on her arm, and somehow, impossibly, I reached the surface.

I took a glorious, too-cold breath of air and leaned back my head, trying to float as I tried to haul her body up, too.

Something tugged her out of my grasp. A wave. A current.

My fingers left her skin. She was pulled back under and gone.

I whirled around, tried peering under into the water. A shark? Had a shark taken her? Or a particularly strong wave? But I'd been gripping her with all of my might, and she was just suddenly...gone.

Something bumped against my leg again.

And I was dragged underwater.

There was a swirl of bubbles, of dark, murky water that was almost impossible to see through. But despite all of that, I could still see what was happening as clear as day. Maybe it was the fear, sharpening my sight. Because the woman underwater had her eyes open. She had dragged me underwater with her hands on my leg, her fingers crawling up my leg to my waist and then my arms, pinning me there as she smiled at me, her eyes flashing.

What was happening?

It was...Mags.

Her grin was too wide, stretching her face out

of shape. Her eyes were open, and I knew she wasn't dead as she turned her face, her mouth opening as she began to draw me towards her slowly. There was a flash of white, in the dark, and I saw something, then, that it was impossible to understand.

Her teeth. They were long. Impossibly long. And sharp. She looked like a shark herself, with dead, doll eyes as she tilted back her head, her mouth wide and open and sharper than anything I could imagine. She drew her head back, and then as fast as a thought, she snaked herself forward and buried her mouth in my neck.

The pain was unbearable. It was cold and hot, all at once. I felt like my flesh was being sawed into. It was too much. I felt her fingers, her sharp, pricking fingers, bury into the flesh of my arms, and her mouth bury into my neck, and I didn't have any thoughts, really. I was too cold, in too much pain and panic, to think anything. I tilted my head back, saw the surface of the dark water far, far above me, and I sunk down below the water with her.

I knew I was going to die.

I knew I was dying.

It's strange how, in moments like that, everything can seem so much sharper, so much clearer. There was a shape above us that I had not noticed before, not until that moment. It was a sort-of human shape, I suppose, though I couldn't make out exact features. I could just make out something that looked, so much, like angel wings, wings that were white-blonde to my eye, though that made no sense.

The last of my breath escaped me. My lungs filled with water.

I closed my eyes.

I wish, I thought. But there was too much to wish for anything specific. For the first time in a very long time, I wanted to live again. I wanted to be alive. I wanted to try with Kane, see if she might be interested. I wanted to try to live a good life. I realized, now, that that's what Anna would have wanted. I'd been so blind. She would have just wanted me to be happy, and I'd been so unhappy for so long. And I wouldn't be able to fix it now.

I wish.

Nothingness rolled over me like the falling night.

And I died.

I was weightless. It was so dark.

And from far, far away, I heard voices.

"What the *hell* were you thinking?" It was so soft, so sibilant, those words, that I almost couldn't hear them. They made everything seem to tremble, though I couldn't feel anything. It was just a knowing. Those words made the ground quake.

"I wanted her. I was hungry." A whining, sibilant sound, those words. The woman who spoke them sounded…well. Frightened.

"Get out of my *sight*."

Silence.

A soft *shushing* sound. Like waves. And, somewhere, the crying of a gull.

A new voice. A gentle woman's voice that sounded deep and wise. And kind: "You know what you have to do, Kane."

A sigh that sounded pained. And then the first

voice said: "Not yet, Branna. I can't. I can't bear to. She hasn't been given a choice. She can't be turned, not like this."

There was a pause. And then a shifting sound, like someone was touching the fabric on another's shoulder. "She's dead, Kane. How else can you bring her back? And you *do* want to bring her back. I can see it in your eyes. I could see it from the first moment she came here. There's something about this one. Something you quite like."

"Branna, I *can't*." There was such anguish in that last word, such pain and sorrow and suffering that it filled me. I wanted to ease that pain. That smooth, dusky voice needed to be spared that pain.

I knew that voice.

"Mags has gone too far. She'll have to be taught a lesson." The gentle voice had turned sharper, now.

"Yes." The voice was a growl.

The gentle voice was thoughtful. "If you won't change the girl, you can try to give her blood back."

"I know."

"You also know that the chance of survival is almost nil."

"I...know."

"Try it this way first. Give her back blood. And if it fails...turn her."

Silence.

The weightlessness began to fade as gravity became pronounced, almost heavy. I began to feel things. Pricking sensations all over my body, like when a foot that's fallen asleep begins to wake up. I began to feel pain, pain filling every part of me like water rushing into a dry room.

Breath filled my aching lungs.

I began to feel...alive.

I took that first great breath of air. It was a terrible, painful breath, the water in my lungs making me cough it out in raspy, heaving spasms. I was being propped up. There was something beneath my upper body, beneath my head that was soft. I tried to open my eyes, but they were so heavy. I struggled with that. I struggled to open them, and I did.

There was a halo of light around the woman holding me. I blinked up at her, and I realized it wasn't a halo of light...it was her hair. Her beautiful white-blonde hair.

Kane Sullivan stared down at me in wonder, eyes wide, mouth open.

Her teeth were sharp. Impossibly sharp. And a single trickle of blood ran down the side of her face from her mouth.

I took another breath of air.

"Hello," whispered Kane, a single small tear tracing down the side of her face as she cradled my head, as I took another deep, ragged breath.

Somewhere, on the edge of the world, the sun peeked over the edge of the horizon. It rose.

The ocean roared behind us, but the sound of my heart overpowered everything as it beat quickly—too quickly.

I knew so very little, in that moment. So very little. And this was it:

I was alive. I knew that. I knew that, impossibly, I'd been dead, and somehow—equally impossibly—I'd been given a second chance. I was *alive*.

Kane stared down at me, her bright blue eyes

flashing. She licked her lips, and a single drop of blood fell from her chin, hanging—as if suspended—in the air before it fell against the cold, bare skin on my shoulder. And against the two gaping wounds there.

And I knew that the woman holding me close, the woman who had saved my life, Kane Sullivan—somehow, impossibly…was a vampire.

Meeting Eternity

-- Eternal Kiss --

I'd just died. And somehow, impossibly...I'd been brought back to life.

Behind us, the ocean boomed against the shore, the brown salt water pounding against the sand and rocks like caramel thunder. The sun had just slipped up and over the edge of the horizon, and it was already swallowed whole, engulfed by the cloud bank that huddled on the edge of the world angrily, like it might storm at any second. It was freezing—I remember that—the cold so absolute in my bones and blood that I wondered if I'd ever stop shaking, if I'd ever be warm again.

But these discomforts seemed so far from me.

Because I was lying on the wet sand in my wet clothes, shaking and coughing, impossibly alive when I should have absolutely been dead.

And I was in the arms of a vampire.

Kane Sullivan stared down at me with her violently blue eyes, the blue so intense and sharp that it seemed to assault me as I lie there, powerless and exhausted and limp in her strong arms. But there was something else behind that power in her eyes. The lone trickle of blood down the side of her face from her full lips, the red contrasting too brightly with the paleness of her skin, the white-gold of her long, wet hair that lay in strands around her face, made me shiver, but then I was drawn back to her eyes again, drawn as if I was compelled by them.

There was power and there was intensity there, yes. And longing. My God, how the longing burned through her so fiercely, I almost stopped breathing again when I gazed at her.

But there was something else in those eyes, too. As I gazed deeply into her dilated black pupils, the black practically engulfing the usual brilliant blue, I saw it flicker again, and I concentrated on it, tried to place it. And then I knew it.

Sadness. Supreme anguish and sadness.

"Are you all right?" she asked me, licking her lips and breathing out, shifting my weight in her arms and against her legs so that she could lift her pale left hand and wipe it over her mouth. If the intent was to get rid of the blood, of the evidence that she was a vampire, it was a wasted effort. Her teeth, teeth I had never seen pointed, now had razor sharp incisors that seemed to glint in the daylight, and the blood smeared on her face like paint.

My breathing came ragged, great gulps of salty air that filled my aching lungs as I stared up at her.

"Rose, are you all right?" came a voice from my left, then. I gazed back, my neck aching, to take in a woman who knelt beside Kane, who seemed familiar to me. Kane wore her usual (albeit soaked through and rumpled) men's suit with the tie, her long, wet, white-blonde hair drawn back into a ponytail and hanging limply over her shoulder, stray strands stuck to the sides of her face. This other woman, too, wore a men's suit, but instead of a tie, there was a smart little black satin bowtie at her neck. Her hair was cut as short as a man's, and lay smoothed and greased against her head, like I imagine men wore it in the fifties. She had a kind face, large brown eyes, a gentle mouth. It was a strange circumstance to meet anyone in, but I liked her on sight.

"I...I think so," I managed, the words coming out like a croak, and then I was coughing again—somehow, impossibly, more seawater spilling up and out of my lungs and mouth. Kane patted my back gently and helped me sit farther up so that the angle to spit out the water was better. I coughed and spat, and finally when I could take another ragged breath in again without coughing, I glanced sidelong at Kane.

She was close enough to kiss, and even though I was soaked through, freezing and bedraggled and had just gotten done spitting out a lungful of seawater, it was a thought I still had.

"What...just happened to me?" I managed to ask, then.

Kane glanced sidelong at the woman, shaking her head almost imperceptibly. And then she stood, and I was standing with her, because I was in her arms, hanging in the protective circle of them like it was a familiar thing.

She lifted me up as if I weighed nothing more than a whisper.

"You have to get in out of the cold, or we'll lose you again," said Kane then, softly, gently, her deep, dark voice quiet as she gazed down at me with those intense, sad eyes.

"I need to know," I croaked out, shaking my head, taking in ragged breaths as I tried to maintain some semblance of breathing. *"What happened to me?"*

"It's no use, Kane—we have to tell her, or she could become frantic," came that deep, gentle voice.

The other woman again. She reached out and brushed her fingers over my shoulder. Kane shook her head, not able to gaze into my eyes as she held me tightly to her. I was aware of her breasts against my side, aware of the muscles in her arms as she held me so lightly. I was aware of the brightness in her eyes, and the curve of her jaw that I couldn't help tracing with my tired eyes. Everything about her drew me in, in a way that I couldn't deny and I certainly couldn't fight against.

Not that I, even then, even in the beginning, would ever have fought against my feelings for Kane Sullivan.

"Very well," Kane whispered, her voice tight and uneasy as she sank down to her knees, gently resting me against the rough sand of the beach, half-leaning against her. The hardness of her muscles contrasted with the softness of her breasts, and I knew exactly how my body was against her, knew it when I closed my eyes—every inch of my skin was extra sensitive in that moment, everything heightened. Above us, too far above us to really make out the sound, I heard the cry of a gull. I *heard* the rush of my own blood, could taste the salt of the water as if someone had poured an entire shaker of salt into my mouth.

I felt...strange.

"But quickly, Branna," Kane hissed up at the woman still standing, the woman's hands on her slight hips. "She's in danger of the elements out here."

"Well, who are we to talk about danger, hm?" asked Branna, the other woman with the close-cropped hair and gentle eyes, as she sank down beside the both of us with an almost teasing smile, an elbow languidly perched on her one knee, the other pressing against the sand. "My name is Branna Sullivan," she told me then, softly, kindly. "And I and Kane—the latter of which I am sure you are most aware—are vampires." She said the word heavily, as if she'd had practice saying it, and as I stared at her wide, brown eyes, I knew she wasn't joking.

I couldn't have acted like this was a farce or some practical joke anyway. I…remembered.

I remembered Mags, under the water, the way her eyes flashed, the way her mouth tore into my skin.

I remembered Kane pulling me from the water.

I remembered her talking with someone else—this woman, I realized, this Branna—as they tried to decide what to do to best save me.

Kane said she was going to give me blood. But that was impossible. There were two gaping wounds in my shoulder, and it's impossible to give blood through a wound and not using a needle…isn't it?

Nothing made sense as I sat on the cold sand, pillowed and in the encircling, protective arms of this woman a few days earlier I hadn't even known, this woman who, from the very first meeting, enthralled and bewitched me in a way I'd never known before.

This woman, Kane Sullivan. Who was a vampire.

Branna cleared her throat, and again I glanced to her, and not to Kane—who wasn't looking at my face anyway. Kane was gazing out to sea as if she had a vast, unanswered question, and only the rolling waves could answer it.

Branna's head was to the side as she glanced me up and down, appraising me. "Is that enough of an answer for now, Miss Clyde? I'm worried you could catch your death. Or…well. Worse."

What's worse than catching my death?

Oh. Yes.

Dying.

I searched Kane's face, trying to get her eyes back to me, but they would not come. I remembered Mags, dragging me under the water, trying to drown me and drain me of blood, I realized, if I was going to believe wholeheartedly that they were, in fact, *vampires*. I stood, then, or tried to, stumbling a little as I propelled myself to feet that felt the pin-and-needle pricking of limbs recently come back to life. And they had, I realized.

All of me had recently come back to life.

"You're vampires," I managed, repeating Branna's sentiment as the two vampires below me remained kneeling and crouching in the sand. Kane's attention was finally back on me, and I hate to admit it…but it made me feel seen. Important. In her gaze, I was alive and I was fully seen, and it rankled me deeply that I wanted her to look at me. That when she wasn't looking at me, when I wasn't the object of her attentions, it smarted.

I'd never been like that. And I didn't want it to start now.

Yes, Kane Sullivan was utterly captivating. Yes, Kane Sullivan had seemingly bewitched me from the first moment I'd met her. But I'd be *damned* if I was desperate for someone's attention—even if that someone was a gorgeous vampire who'd just saved me from dying.

"So, Mags was just…going to eat me up for a morning snack?" I spluttered, trying to draw my ragged and torn garments (what had once, I supposed, been my pajama top—my coat was long gone, lost to the waves). "Is that how you all are?" I managed, taking a deep breath, trying to quell hysteria. Cool, appraising anger began to move through me, then, replacing the franticness. I much preferred the anger.

But with it came a strange...side effect. As I stood over the two women, as I tried to draw the scraps closer around my shoulders (I was the type of bone-deep chilled that made me wonder if I might ever be warm again), I began to realize that every one of my senses was much sharper, brighter. Honestly, it felt like getting drunk...but in reverse. When I get tipsy (or, let's be honest, completely smashed), everything around me seems to be going much too fast, and it's all muddled. Here and now, everything was completely and crystalline clear. I could hear the sound of particles of sand moving against other particles, the scuttle of tiny crab legs farther down the beach. If I glanced out to sea, I could make out the shape of fish miles from shore.

"What's happening to me?" I asked, marveling, staring down at my hands. I could hear the thrum of a million miles of veins, could hear the individual cells of blood moving in me.

"I gave you some of my blood," said Kane, unfolding and standing in one smooth, graceful motion. She glanced down at me, then, her head to the side, her arms folded carefully, and her feet hip-width apart. She looked at ease, but I could sense how she could move, so quickly, in a heartbeat. I felt that I, too, could have caught a falling wine glass perfectly or could sidestep an oncoming car. It was a strange, exhilarating sensation, rushing through me. A powerful one. "I gave you blood back," said Kane, then, her nostrils flaring a little as she sniffed the air. "The blood of a vampire is...powerful," she said, letting the word dangle between us. "You will have some heightened sensations for a few days as the blood moves through you."

"You had to give me blood," I said, words flat, "because Mags took most of mine."

"You would have died if Kane had not sensed it," said Branna, standing too, brushing off the knees of her once-immaculate pants. The sound of the grains of sand falling to the beach sounded like pebbles plinking against one another. "She came immediately to...well. Save you." She gazed into my eyes with her own unblinking ones, the brown so deep and dark, they seemed to swallow me for a moment.

"Are you like her?" I asked, then. But I wasn't asking Branna. I turned to Kane, I always seemed to be turning to Kane, but I couldn't help it. There was something about her body, her face...every part of her, inside and out, that seemed to incite in me a longing that my heart and body obeyed, even if my head did not. Okay—to be perfectly truthful, my head wanted to obey, too. But I was having a hard time letting it. She gazed down at me, her blue eyes flashing, so bright, so piercing as they seemed to see down and into the deepest, darkest parts of me.

"I was, once, like her," Kane murmured then, the words spilling past her full lips so softly, but I could hear them as clearly as if she'd whispered into my ear, her mouth against my skin. "But I'm not like Mags anymore," she continued, her face growing hard, her eyes distant as she thought of Mags. "And I haven't been. Not for a long time. I'm sorry, what she did to you...it was unthinkable. She will be taught a lesson." Her jaw clenched at that, and I couldn't help it: I shivered, the shake moving from my legs up to my shoulders in one powerful motion. I breathed out, placed my hand over my heart.

"Am I going to..." I searched my head, thinking back on all of the ridiculous pop culture notions I had about vampires. I was, admittedly, taking this much better than expected, but dying and coming back to life gives you a pretty strange perspective on things. "Am I going to become like you?" I asked, looking deeply into her eyes, trying to see if I could find some sort of admission, some sort of flinch to my question. But she gazed into my eyes unwavering.

"No," she said, finally, heavily.

Kane turned from me, as Branna continued to gaze at me, one brow up, the corners of her mouth turning up, too, as she considered me.

"Do you *want* to become like us, Rose?" she asked softly.

Kane stiffened at that, gazing at the other woman with those sharp, piercing eyes, but Branna was still considering me, gazing me up and down as if she was weighing pros and cons in her head.

"I don't...I don't...this is too much," I managed then, my head beginning to whirl. The sounds of the ocean, of the world around me, the scents and sights of it, were too heightened and sharpened, and I knew how much I was in over my head then.

"You need to rest," said Branna softly, soothingly, as Kane stepped forward, the nearness of her body making my own curve toward her. I felt so lightheaded, suddenly, and I seemed to be falling, but there was solidity all around me as Kane lifted me up, holding me close to her.

"I'll take you back up to the hotel," whispered Kane into my ear then, as darkness began to rise in me.

And then, right before I lost consciousness, and so softly I might have imagined it, Kane breathed: "I'll keep you safe."

When I woke up, it was difficult for me to remember anything other than the fact that I was probably late for my shift.

My shift at the Sullivan Hotel.

The...Sullivan Hotel.

Kane Sullivan.

Kane Sullivan is a vampire.

I blinked and stared up at my ceiling as all the details began to spill back into me, one by one. If Kane and Branna and Mags were all vampires—and I remembered, now, that the reason Branna had seemed familiar to me was because I'd seen her in the drawing room the previous day, the room with the wreaths of smoke, filled with women who had not, not even remotely, looked related, but who all seemed to bear the last name of "Sullivan." I'd wondered, then (jokingly), if "Sullivan" was a code word I'd never heard for "lesbians." Gwen had, after all, seemed to be under the suspicion that every single one of the Sullivans seemed to be attracted to women.

But the reason none of the Sullivan women looked similar or related, I realized, was that they all *were* probably unrelated...and all vampires.

I breathed in and out, pushing down my inherent fear that seemed to rise in me, making my breath come short. It was stupid to be afraid of them.

Yes, Mags had wanted to drain me dry, and as I replayed the moments in the ocean, trying to save what I had believed to be a drowning woman, I realized that she'd probably used that as a ruse to lure me out into the water. Great. So, it seemed that she'd actually been *hunting* me. If that was any indication, then yes—I should absolutely be afraid of them. Utterly, mortally terrified.

But as I closed my eyes, weakly leaning back on my too-plump pillow and taking deep, calming breaths, the vision of Kane Sullivan came unbidden into my head. The beautiful skin of her neck that led down to the starched white collar of her suit, the perfect, simple knot of the tie at the delicious curve of her throat as it spilled down onto white skin that led to other, more beautiful things that I could only imagine. The curve of her jaw, that handsome curve that was so strong, those full lips and handsome nose and her eyes, my God, her eyes...

I wasn't in any danger from Kane.

Maybe. *Possibly.*

And if I *was* in danger from her...it didn't seem like such a terrible danger after all.

Again, my head began to argue with my body and my heart. My body that was completely and unapologetically attracted to that bewitching creature.

And my heart that seemed utterly convinced that I knew her from somewhere. And that I loved her.

I stopped at that as I considered it. My eyes sprung open, and I sat up so quickly that my heart began pounding even before I thought about all of those implications. I'd just *met* Kane Sullivan. We'd had some intense encounters, and I couldn't deny my attraction to her, it was true, but *love?* It seemed impossible.

But...hadn't vampires seemed impossible, just last night?

No. No. Absolutely not. I did not love Kane Sullivan.

But you're falling for her, my heart argued softly with my head.

I couldn't deny it. That much was true.

And that fact made things *tremendously* complicated. Because not only was I falling in love with my new boss, the owner of this big, sprawling hotel where I currently found myself employed...but—perhaps the most pressing thing—I was falling in love with a *vampire*.

To this day, I don't truly understand how easily I believed the idea of vampires, that they existed and were real and owned the hotel in which I worked. Perhaps it was the fact that, all my life, I'd just been boring Rose Clyde who still hoped and wished desperately for something wonderful and interesting to happen to her. Perhaps it was because I was so attracted to Kane that I was willing to believe she was anything she wanted to be.

But as I thought about it that evening, stretched out on my bed in my room on the fifth floor of the Sullivan Hotel, the sunset spilling into my window, burnished light lengthening the shadows on the old, well-worn floorboards, I felt a strangeness uncurl in my belly, as if some memory had been loosed and would come back to me at the perfect moment, when it was good and ready.

I suppose that the reason that I was accepting this all so easily was that it was, strangely...familiar.

I got up, then. I was restless, and the wounds

in my neck throbbed, a deep-seated ache that made my jaw clench, that made me want to outpace it, if I could. I walked over to the far wall, where a gilt, antique mirror hung, its gold frame ornamented with a bunch of little metal roses. I reached out and touched one, my finger brushing against the cool patina as I peeled back the throat of my new pajama top (who had put this pajama top on me? I blushed a little at the thought) with my other hand, and stared at the wounds.

Before, that morning, I could see that these wounds had been ragged, bloody, torn flesh that showed muscle and blood. Mags had not been gentle. But now, they were almost completely, and impossibly…healed. Tiny pinpricks were in my shoulder, a little red, but hardly swollen, and nothing else besides. They still hurt terribly, but I had to admit that it wasn't so much pain as an ache, the type of ache that happens a week or so after a hard injury.

I couldn't possibly have healed that quickly, even if I'd been out for days, lying in bed unconscious almost a week, and I had the feeling that all of the strange events had taken place only that morning. I couldn't have healed in a day. It wasn't possible.

I set my jaw, then. I saw myself in the mirror, long, red hair unkempt and tumbling over my shoulders, my brown eyes wide and resolute as I stared at myself, stared deeply into my own eyes at the recognition that registered there.

It was impossible, yes.
And yet, it had also happened.
There was a knock at my door.

I warily glanced sidelong at that door, brows raised. I wanted time to process everything, figure out exactly what was happening, but life goes on, and we

93

don't always get the time we need.

I crossed the room, placed my hand on the doorknob, took a deep breath, and opened it.

Branna stood there, wearing the men's suit and bow tie and a conciliatory smile, a bottle of wine dangling from one hand, the other holding a tray with a silver platter and silver cover on it, effortlessly aloft.

"I thought you might be hungry," she said soothingly, her smile deepening. "Mind if I come in?"

My mind threw out the very first thing I thought of. "Is this like in Buffy?" I managed, crossing my arms and frowning a little. "Do I have to invite you into my room for you to be able to enter?"

She chuckled at that, a rich, throaty laugh that, despite myself, I found myself answering with a chuckle of my own.

"That's *television* vampires," she said, raising a brow as she cocked her head to the side a little, her deep brown eyes flashing with bemusement. "Also, I *do* live in this building, too—so no."

I stepped aside, ushering her forward with my arm and closing the door behind her as she set the large tray on the table beside my chair, lifting the silver dome off the tray with a flourish.

"*Voila!* Cheese lasagna—vegetarian, don't worry—broccoli au gratin, and french fries covered in cheese. Gwendolyn did inform us that you are a fan of *fromage*." She was grinning as she indicated the chair. "Please, sit—you must be famished."

And it was true—the second she removed the dome from the tray, my stomach gave a pitiful growl in protest. Suddenly, I was so hungry that the mountains of gooey cheese-coated things on the tray didn't even seem like it would be enough to satisfy me. I sat down, sinking into the blue plush of the chair as I regarded Branna with a raised brow.

"You need to eat to keep up your strength—the blood going through you is going to take a few days to become fully human. Until then, your senses will continue to be heightened, and you'll be...hungrier than usual," said Branna, leaning against the post of the bed as she appraised me. "How are you feeling?"

"Achey, but okay," I told her, lifting a forkful of gooey noodle to my mouth. The lasagna was the best I'd ever had the pleasure of tasting, and my eyes rolled back into my head a little as I breathed out with a sigh of happiness.

"Rose, I have to tell you," said Branna, then, leaning not on the post, but on the edge of the bed as she settled, crossing her legs in a picture of ease. "Mags would have finished you. Killed you. I don't tell you this to alarm you," she said, shaking her head and raising her hand when she saw my fork pause, "but to...well..." She ran that hand through her hair, then, the greased strands of it not moving an inch. "Normally, we don't feed so...gruesomely as Mags would have done. We feed on willing...well, we call them 'donors,' or we get blood from other sources. We don't *need* the blood of humans to survive, no matter what the movies or books have told you," she said with a small smile. "So, when we feed, it's quite a dainty affair. We don't leave corpses." Her voice took on a sharp tone, and I glanced up, again my fork hovering in mid-air. Her eyes, so bright and warm, flashed dangerously just then. "Mags was very out of line, and I wanted you to know that you have nothing to fear from her, going forward. But there is the slight problem..." Branna trailed off, her head to the side as she considered me. "You know now what we are."

I took a sip of water, unsure of what to say. Was Branna implying that others *didn't* know? That it was a secret? I could imagine that something like this would be a fact they very much didn't want to get out. But I wasn't that kind of person. I didn't really gossip, and I didn't go around telling important secrets that weren't mine to reveal to random people. Even if the secret in question was about vampires not exactly being fiction.

"I won't say anything," I told her, setting the fork down beside my mostly empty plate. "Is that what you're worried of?"

"We've lived here for a hundred years in peace," said Branna softly, one brow up. "Not to put too fine a point on it, my dear, but by Kane saving you, she has jeopardized all of that."

I don't know why, but those words stung me. "I won't say anything," I repeated, but I tried to see it from her point of view, too. What reason would she have to believe me? I just felt, in that moment, that she did have a reason, but I would never have been able to tell you what it was. It was just a feeling, and it went as quickly as it came.

"Before I was turned, a very long time ago, I had a gift as a human that I was able to keep as a vampire. I'm what is best understood by the word 'empath,'" said Branna then, standing in one smooth motion. "I can feel what you're feeling, if you'll let me. May I?"

I didn't exactly know what I was agreeing to, but I nodded, giving her my hand, as she seemed to be indicating by holding her palm out to me. She held my hand gently, delicately, her eyes glazing for a moment as she stared at the space over my head.

Branna's breath caught a little, after a heartbeat, and she dropped my palm as if it had stung her.

I stood, all in a rush, because in that heartbeat, her pupils had dilated, and her incisors had seemed to…well. They'd *grown*.

"I'm sorry," she said, shaking her head for a moment, licking her lips and closing her mouth. When she straightened, then, her incisors were perfectly normal, and her eyes were back to the same warm, rich brown. "Excuse me, please—I was startled," she said with a polite smile, but there was a questioning glance behind it. "When I touched you, I felt that you spoke the truth about not wishing to reveal us. I don't believe you'll tell anyone, and when we have the meeting to decide what to do with you, I shall tell them that fact."

"Wait…what?" I said, stepping forward, touching her sleeve as she walked past, on her way to the door. My heart was pounding so quickly it seemed to be a roar in my ears. "First off…you're having a *meeting* about me? What you're going to *do* with me? And then…" I took a gulp of air, searched her eyes. "What else did you see?"

She shook her head, not meeting my glance. She looked tired. "Rose, please…"

I tightened my hold on her sleeve, and she paused with a sigh.

"I've read a lot of people in my very long life," she said then, quietly. "And I remember every one. And when I first touched you, it seemed that I'd…well, that'd I'd read you before."

"That's not possible," I said, swallowing, my heart building to a crashing roar. "I've never met you before."

She searched my eyes then for a long moment. "You're right," she laughed a little, shaking her head. "We haven't met, have we? It's been a long day," she said, and the words sounded exhausted. "I must just be tired."

I felt uneasy about that, but I didn't know what else to say. "And the...the meeting?"

"That's tonight. Now, really," she said, searching my face again. "We're not going to do anything to you, Rose, so please don't be afraid—you have no reason to fear us, as difficult as that must be to believe, considering what Mags did to you this morning," she whispered, then, voice soft. "But we all must decide if you should stay at the Sullivan Hotel or not."

Her words made me speechless for only a second. "Why don't I get a choice in that?" I asked, then, anger pulsing through me again. "I feel that I should get a say in that decision. I did *nothing*. I didn't *want* to be attacked. Why would I have to go?"

She searched my face, eyes wide. "The question is, Rose, after everything you've found out this day...why don't you *want* to go?"

I took a step back. She was right, of course. To put it bluntly, I'd just realized that I was currently living in a big house full of *vampires*. And one of those vampires, that morning, had definitely tried to kill me. And she'd still be living in this house with me, too—I doubt they'd gotten rid of her. They were a "family," after all.

But, for all of that, I knew with my whole heart that I couldn't leave the Sullivan Hotel.

"Can I come to this meeting?" I asked her, my mouth suddenly dry.

She hesitated for a long moment, then nodded slightly.

"I'm going to get changed," I said, resolve making my words not shake, courage building in my heart. "Can you wait outside for me? I'll only be half a moment."

Branna bit her lip with a long sigh. And agreed.

What do you wear to a vampire meeting?

I opted for red.

"You look…nice," said Branna with a chuckle, and a shake of her head when I exited my bedroom door. She'd waited for me in the hallway, lounging against the wall as if she hadn't had a care in the world. Branna was very easy about everything, the way she pushed off the wall, the way she inclined her head to me appreciatively, glancing me up and down in my red dress (it was hardly revealing, but it was a nice dress, and it showed off my curves, and red seemed like an appropriate—albeit cliché—color to be around vampires in) and offering her arm to me in one smooth motion.

I'd been wondering about something, and now seemed like the best time to say it of any. Here's another thing about almost dying: it makes you pretty bold.

"Branna, are all of the vampires here lesbian?" I asked, my mouth going dry as I said the words, and they were pretty pointed, but if I was going to be kicked out of the house, it'd be nice to know at least what I'd been missing.

Branna's mouth quirked sideways at that, and

she suppressed a chuckle as I slipped my arm through her proffered one, resting my fingers on the top of her forearm gently.

"Please—call me Bran," she said, voice light. "And though that word, 'lesbian,' is relatively new, in the grand scheme of history...yes, I suppose that's what you'd call us," she said, inclining her head toward me so that the word "yes" drifted with warm, sweet breath over my skin. I shuddered at that, my pulse racing. Branna looked ahead, then, down the hallway as we walked together. "Kane started the...family," said Branna softly, frowning a little, "a very long time ago. She wanted to find people who were like her. It's lonely, this existence, and she didn't want to be alone. So we found others who matched our ideals, who, like us, preferred the company of the...sweeter sex." Her warm, rich voice elicited another throaty chuckle. "And, believe it or not, I know your next question, my dear. No, we don't usually prefer the romantic company of other vampires, so no, we don't perform mass orgies in the halls. That's not how this family was built or why we are together, for frequent, easy and constant sexual congress."

"I wasn't going to ask *that*," I said with a flush, but I'd been about to ask something similar. Vampires and sex, after all, seemed to be inextricably linked if pop culture was anything to go on. "I'm just so curious about all of you," I told her, then, which was very true. "Are you undead? Are you dead? Are you cursed? Do you have souls? I'm sorry," I realized, all in a rush, as she cast a sidelong, bemused glance at me, "if any of this is offensive. I just don't know what's real, or what's based on things like television and books and stuff like *Dracula*."

"Ah, *Dracula*," said Branna with a chuckle. "Did you know that its author, Bram Stoker, actually stole most of his material? Ah, rather he was *inspired* by another work of fiction. It came much earlier than *Dracula*, but no one much knows of it. It's called *Carmilla*. Have you ever heard of it?"

I shook my head, but she didn't allow me to feel ignorant. "Don't worry, *ma chere*, not many people have." She inclined her head toward me, the slant of her mouth charming. "Though it is, I must admit, a very sweet little book. It is about a vampire woman," she said, with twinkling eyes, "who loves another woman with all of her heart."

I stared at her in open shock (if it came before *Dracula*, this made the book pretty old—and it contained lesbians? Would wonders never cease...) and she nodded with a laugh. "Though, I must admit, it doesn't get the science of vampirism right either, it's a very lovely tale." She cocked her head, considering my questions. "Now, to answer you—we have never died, no. We're still very much alive, but we're not truly *immortal*, as you consider that definition. Vampires simply live for a very long time. We are not cursed, and if you believe that human beings have souls, then yes— we have souls, too. Vampirism is a sort of...super virus," she explained, anticipating my next string of questions. "It's transmitted with blood, but quite a bit of blood, and you must be almost entirely drained in order for it to work. A vampire must give most of his or her blood to you once you've been almost completely drained. Being a vampire makes you stronger, faster, more powerful than a human being, with a much-extended lifespan, and you crave blood. And that's really it. We don't sleep in coffins. But the sunlight does affect us as a side effect of the virus—we can be in it, but not for very long, or we become weak." She laughed. "Garlic sadly doesn't work on us, and yes—you can see us in mirrors. A lot of people built a lot of superstitions around us, because, of course, people rising from their graves is a somewhat off-putting thing. Humans fear death, and we don't have mastery over it, but I suppose it looks like we do. Thus we were feared, and stories tend to grow around that thing you are afraid of."

I pondered all of this for a long moment, turning things over in my heart. "Are all vampires like you? Like the Sullivans?" I wasn't certain how to phrase it, but it seemed to me from how Kane had been so angry about Mags attacking me that they weren't any sort of blood-thirsty, human-killing vampires, but I didn't know if this was true of *all* vampires.

Branna shook her head, her mouth tightening. "No. We're peaceful. We want to be left alone, live out our lives in peace, spend time together in friendship and…love." She looked at me quickly before continuing: "but others do not want the same things. There are many vampires who seek to destroy and kill. So no. Like all humans, all vampires are different."

I was awash with a million more questions, but we'd found our way to the ornate door carved round with cherubs and vines and violets and I knew it led to the drawing room I'd been taken to yesterday. I straightened my shoulders as Branna took a step forward, her hand poised to knock on the door.

But Dolly opened it, Branna's hand falling on air.

Dolly's bright blonde curls danced around her sweet, cherubic face as she took in the sight of both of us, her pretty pink dress swirling about her knees, her pink high-heels the exact same color as the fluffy skirt of the dress. Her cherry-red mouth was pouting, and she looked right past Branna at me, her eyes growing wider as she took me in.

"Bran, you're late!" she chided, and Branna's smile grew wider and more indulgent as she stepped forward, placing a chaste kiss on the side of Dolly's mouth. But Dolly didn't even really acknowledge her. She was still staring at me.

"Are you…are you all right?" she asked, pulling me into the room with a gentle hand before shutting the door behind me with a soft *click*.

"She's fine, Doll," said a gravelly voice in the smoke-shrouded room. A woman was sitting at the same card table that Dolly and I had played gin rummy at just yesterday—but it seemed like a lifetime ago now. She was shuffling the cards, and, as I watched, began to deal herself a game of solitaire. Her full lips seemed like they were stretched into a permanent frown, and her bleached-blonde hair was carefully slicked into a pompadour at the front of her head. She wore a loose-fitting blazer, and the top six buttons on her creamy shirt beneath it were unbuttoned, so that I could see the gray sports bra under it. This woman was hard butch all the way, and just seemed hard in general as she glanced up at me, her dark eyes flashing. "She's still kicking, isn't she? She's fine."

"Jane, Mags could have *killed* her," said Dolly with wide eyes, making small, reassuring circles with the palm of her hand on the small of my back.

"And she didn't, did she?" asked Jane, kicking back and balancing the chair on its back two legs, regarding me with a tilt of her head and quick eyes. "So

103

give it a rest. God, you'd think the rest of you had never had a drink from a pretty girl before."

"Not like that, Jane," said Branna lightly, but there was a bit of an edge to her voice.

I felt eyes on me, then. And there were other women in the room, it was true, but I knew the weight of these eyes, a familiar weight that made butterflies beat against my heart. I glanced to the back of the room, to the wide fireplace that smoldered, its marble mantle carved with vines and violets and devilish looking cherubs.

She stood there, leaning against the mantle, her hands curled loosely in her pockets, her long white-blonde ponytail curved over one shoulder, and a cigarette dangling out of perfect, full lips.

Kane.

Her bright blue eyes had me in their sights, and the way she gazed at me...it made me shiver. There was a magnetic quality to that gaze, and I was pulled by it, tugged by it, drawn by my heart all the way across the room, until I hadn't even realized that I'd come the full way, and I was standing before her, close enough to touch.

Her gaze raked me up and down, taking in the dress, my body, and my skin pricked at that, goosebumps rising to be so wholly appraised in a single glance. Her blue eyes flashed, darkening, and she took a single graceful step toward me. She set her hand purposefully on the mantle behind me, then, and she towered over me, this handsome, intense creature, as she stared down at me with unblinking blue eyes that seemed electric in the dimly lit room. She stood close enough to me that when I breathed out, then, my breath came between us like smoke. She was so cold that if I touched her, I'd be burned by it. But I wanted to touch her just the same.

"Are you all right?" she asked me, then, and her voice was a low growl as she offered the question. Yes. I was all right. But as I stared up into her eyes, I knew that I wasn't really. I was completely bewitched by her. And that wasn't really all right, was it.

Someone cleared her throat behind us, and Kane straightened a little, her eyes flashing as she gazed past my shoulder to the woman standing behind us. Branna.

"Rose, I feel that I should introduce all of us, if I might," said Branna, then. There was a violin dangling from her hand, just then, and I remembered her as the woman who had played for us yesterday. How could I forget? But everything else faded away as I gazed around at the assembled women—noting, with a fair amount of relief, that Mags was not among them—realizing in one odd, surreal moment, that I was standing in a room full of vampires. Who were all staring at me.

"Full introductions would be wonderful," I said with a quavering breath.

She didn't hesitate. "I am Branna—call me Bran, though," said Bran with a wink. "You've met Kane and Dolly...and, most recently Jane." Still at the table and still leaning her chair back on two legs, Jane threw me a salute. "But this lovely here, is Cecelia." Bran indicated an intense, serious-looking young woman who leaned back in her chair, her arms crossed at the waist. She wore a buttoned dress shirt, with a loose tie, the top few buttons open at the neck, and her tie dangling. Her hair was pinned up in a no-nonsense but pretty updo, a few stray brown curls escaping it.

Cecelia seemed to be able to stare right through me, and I felt completely exposed to her. I shivered a little. "This here, if you remember, is Victoria." Bran indicated the stunning black woman who raised her ever-present martini glass to me, giving me a wink, her Elvis-style hair tilting a little to the side, her purple sheath dress shimmery today. "This is Luce." This woman was taller than even Kane, her flowing red hair down her back like a waterfall of satin, a silver band of metal around her bare upper right arm twinkling in the firelight as she gave me a fierce, wild grin. "And *this*," said Bran, clapping her hand on the last woman's shoulder, "is Thomasina—but she'd despair if you called her that. So call her Tommie."

Tommie was lounging backward, her elbow on the back of her old wooden folding chair, her shoulders curved away from me under her immaculate white dress shirt, nonchalant and easy. She had chin-length black hair that curved out from her jaw at a sharp angle and she was wearing a floppy old fedora, a black that had become gray from age, though she, herself, appeared to be in her twenties (though I half-wondered if she was actually much older than the fedora itself). She gazed up at me from under the brim of the hat, just then, and her grin was lazy, wide and it took my breath away. She didn't glance at me for long, but she gave me an appraising gaze, too, raking over my body with her green eyes that seemed to be able to see right through the fabric of my dress. I actually blushed when Tommie looked at me, but then she went back to her conversation with Luce, and I was just left with my blush.

A cold few fingers curling around my elbow made me turn a little, and Kane was there, glancing down into my face, gazing deeply into my eyes in the dim light as if she was searching for something. "Have you considered what happened to you this morning?" she asked me then, quietly.

Branna stepped forward, shaking her head. "I read her. She won't tell anyone about the vampirism, at least—that's not her intention," she said, warm brown eyes on mine.

Kane glanced up at her, and then back down to me, taking another deep pull of her cigarette before flicking the ash off with long, graceful fingers. Again, I realize that cigarettes are terrible for you, no one should use them, I know, I *know*, but when Kane took a pull on it, it was *so* damn sexy.

And now that I knew she was a vampire, I realized that cigarettes probably didn't affect her like they did humans. So I no longer felt quite so terrible for thinking she was incredibly attractive when she smoked.

"It's not just about that, though, is it, Bran?" asked Jane, her chair *thumping* down in an instant. She rolled onto her feet, stretching overhead. Her permanent frown seemed to deepen. "If she spills the beans *anytime*, *anywhere*, whether she intended to or no, we're in jeopardy."

"But I won't—" I began, but the door to the room opened, just then, flinging wide open.

And there, framed in the entrance to the room, the setting sun behind her outlining every one of her dangerous curves, stood Mags.

She was still stunning, still lethally beautiful with her round, curving hips sheathed in a pencil skirt today, her breasts hardly concealed by the vintage cream-colored top that followed her lines perfectly. Her shimmering black hair was swept into an up-do that seemed to sparkle with crystals, and her makeup was retro and flawless—honestly, she looked like a movie star from the fifties about to walk down the red carpet.

But when she gazed at me, just then, her eyes flashing like a lioness who's picked out the weak zebra from the watering hole to hunt later...and she didn't really look like a movie star anymore.

She looked dangerous.

"Mags..." Dolly's voice was gentle, but there was a surprising hard edge to it. "You know you're not to come here tonight—"

"Last I checked, *Doll*," Mags snarled as she prowled into the room, the door thudding shut behind her, "it's my house too."

I didn't even register the fact that Kane was moving—she was at my side, and then, in an instant, she was in front of me, between me and Mags, her hand behind her back, and her fingers curving and cold around my wrist, but the pressure there a reassuring weight.

"Leave," whispered Kane. It was only a single word, but it seemed, for half a heartbeat, that the red and black checkered floor beneath us seemed to shudder a little with the gravity of the syllable.

Mags paused in her approach of us, paused with one pointed toe before her, on unreasonably tall stilettos, and the other beneath her. She paused as still as a mannequin, and then a very slow, lazy grin began to spread across her face, twisting her full red lips.

"All right," she said, tracing her finger over the curve of her shoulder and down her neck, toward her collarbone as she looked past Kane and directly into my eyes. The ruby-red nails on her hand seemed to prick her skin, because she had two little wounds on her neck, then...exactly where mine were. I shuddered as her smile turned malicious, and she turned on her heel, practically flouncing back toward the door.

It slammed shut behind her.

"Branna," said Kane softly, quietly, "please follow her and make certain that she obeys the letter of her punishment."

Bran turned to me, brows up. "She has to leave the house for a week," Bran told me with a careful shrug.

I don't really believe in capital punishment, and I certainly don't believe in punishment in general...but I'd also never been almost drained dry by a vampire who sought me out for a nonconsensual drink and purposefully hunted me down...and apparently didn't have a single shred of remorse for either of these things. I honestly didn't even know what it was about me that she found so utterly repulsive. From the very first moment that I'd met Mags Sullivan, she'd seemed to have it out for me, and I didn't know why.

But it was also incredibly unnerving, knowing she was just going to be gone for a week. And what then?

"But...doesn't it seem like she's going to try to bite me again?" I managed to keep my voice from shaking, but just barely. Bran was already out the door, it closing softly behind her as she followed Mags, and Kane turned her full attentions to me.

"This is her warning, this week away from the safety, companionship and community of her home here at the Sullivan Hotel. To bite you again, to threaten you in any way, would mean complete and irrevocable expulsion from us. And I promise you: she doesn't want that," said Kane's voice, still dark and growling, but softer as she gazed down at me. I realized, then, that Kane's fingers were still at my elbow, still curled gently over my skin, still cold as ice. She seemed to notice it at the exact same moment, too, and she let go of me, taking a step back, and lifting her cigarette, took a pull and flicked the ash away.

"We need to discuss if she's leaving or not," said Jane, then, nodding toward me and crossing her arms. She'd sunk down into her chair again, but the way she looked at me...I realized she didn't trust me. And probably wanted me gone.

"Let's not be hasty," said Dolly, stepping forward briskly so that her pink skirt flared out around her. "Yes, Rose knows about us. But she isn't like Betty—"

"Let's be *honest:* we thought *Betty* wouldn't be like Betty," said Jane, pulling a hand over her face for a heartbeat before sighing and leaning back again.

"Who was Betty?" I asked, worrying at my lip with my teeth.

"Betty was the only other employee of the Sullivan Hotel who found out about us. She worked here in the forties," said Dolly, pulling at one of her curls alongside her face so that it elongated like a spring. "Um...she fell in love with—"

"She doesn't need to know all the details," said Jane with a growl. I realized with a start that her full lips were up and over her teeth in a snarl, and her eyes had darkened...and her fangs had grown demonstrably. I took a step back, but Jane wasn't looking at me—she was looking at Dolly.

"Well, anyway," said Dolly hastily, with a quick, conciliatory smile as she spread her pink-nailed hands.

"She fell in love with someone *here* and when things didn't really go as planned, she threatened to tell everyone."

"What happened to Betty?" I asked, breathing out. I was close enough to Kane and her cold body that this breath hung suspended in the air, like I stood outside on a winter's night, even though I actually stood in front of the fire. I felt the cold length of her behind me, could see her out of the corner of my eye toss the stub of her cigarette into the blaze as she leaned against the mantle again, her eyes not on Dolly. But on me.

"She was out on a boat. She drowned," said Dolly, her pretty face contorted in a grimace.

I stared at her.

"It wasn't...it wasn't foul play," said Dolly quickly. A little *too* quickly. "But the facts of the matter are that she would have gone to the authorities and the town with the knowledge that we're vampires. And we'd have to leave. Everything we've built would be destroyed."

I'd been thinking it for a while, so I finally said it: "What I don't understand is how you can stay in one place for so long anyway," I told her with a shake of my head. "Eternal Cove looks like it's a pretty small town—don't people get suspicious?"

"We trade out the task of figurehead of ownership of the hotel every generation or so, and we're not seen in the town that much," said Victoria, taking a sip of her martini and leaning back in her plush chair, her hand resting lightly on her bare thigh. The slit on that dress went *spectacularly* high. "To be perfectly honest," she said, leaning forward, her red mouth curling upwards, her dark eyes dancing, "I don't think our dear Rose here is going to say anything. I

111

think she should stay with us. It'd be a shame to send her packing—she *did* just arrive."

"All the more reason not to trust her," Jane rumbled.

"I don't *want* to go," I said then, my hands curling into fists at my sides. I swallowed, tried to find something tactful to say...and failed. "I didn't volunteer to be tricked, almost drowned, bitten, *drained*. I didn't *want* this knowledge that you're all vampires. But now that I know, I don't see anything different about me. I need a job. I'm a good worker, and I'll do my best here. Just because you're vampires...it doesn't change anything." That sounded weak, even to my ears, and Jane chuckled—though it didn't sound at all humorous—as she pushed her chair back and balanced it on the back two legs again.

"Right," she said, with a snort. "You're in a house full of vampires, and you're not the least bit alarmed by that fact? Every human *fears* us, Rose. We're predators, pure and simple. We're the stuff of *nightmares*."

Kane straightened at that, and I couldn't help it—I didn't want to see her out of the corner of my eye, I wanted to be looking at her headlong. I turned just as Branna slipped back into the room, leaning against the door as she shut it, her arms crossed.

"I want her to stay," said Kane softly.

The room stilled.

Kane stepped forward, but she didn't look at me. She moved past me without even acknowledging me, though her long ponytail drifted over my bare arm as she stepped past—it felt like silk, and I shivered as she moved, close enough to touch, but I did not touch her. She slipped past Bran, and then she was out of the room, and into the corridor. The door shut with a soft *click* behind her.

"Well, I suppose that's that," said Dolly uncertainly as she gazed at the shut door.

"Great," muttered Jane with an eye roll, turning her attentions back to her game of solitaire.

Branna appraised me with a single brow up as I stood, alone and unsure by the fire, shifting from foot to foot like I was the new kid in second grade. I felt awkward and out of place, and my skin pricked to attention, all my thoughts revolving around the fact that Kane had left, and I very much wanted to go after her. That is, until Tommie stood.

She'd been silent during the proceedings, but she'd been watching me from under the brim of the old fedora. I was awash with too many feelings, too many uncertainties. Why had Kane said that? What did she mean? Did she feel this strange thing growing between us? I was desperately attracted to her, but I fought against that. I didn't want to be *desperate* about anything, but every single time I was around Kane Sullivan, I seemed to lose all of my reasoning abilities in favor of my heart pounding much too quickly, and my body curving toward her like I was compelled by her form.

Tommie strode over to me, her hands in her pants pockets, her head cocked a little. She was lithe and lean and seemed to be in complete control of every inch of her body. She leaned her shoulder against the mantle, gave me another once over, her green eyes flashing as her lips turned up at the corners. "Been a strange day, huh?" Her voice was warm and low, but there was a little laughter to it, too. I glanced sidelong to her, turning to the fire as I did it, holding out my hands to the blaze. I felt cold.

"Yeah," I managed, biting my lip as I breathed out.

"It's going to start getting stranger. Just a bit of friendly advice," said Tommie, her brows up as she glanced down at the fire, too. "The guests are going to start arriving tonight for the Conference."

"Conference?" I asked her, turning to look at her. She was so beautiful. "Beautiful" would actually not be the exact right word for Tommie. She exuded sexuality, but was masculine, too. She was handsome, absolutely handsome, but there was a hardness to the glint in her eyes, the turn of her smile. It was incredibly difficult not to be attracted to her on sight, and if I was being completely honest with myself...I was. It wasn't like with Kane, though. Tommie was handsome, yes...but there was something about Kane that drew me to her. It was different.

"The vampires, the world over, meet once a year. It's called 'the Conference.' They chose to meet here this year. They meet here every couple of years or so, because it's an out of the way place, and safe from most curious bystanders. So the hotel will be practically *filled* with vampires," said Tommie, her mouth twitching into a smile again as my heart began to beat faster—not from attraction, but from fear. "The thing about the Conference, of course," she whispered, leaning closer to me as she grinned wickedly, "is that there are going to be many vampires here who aren't really like us."

"Like you?" I breathed.

"Let's just say they don't have the same *values* as us. And they don't look at humans the same way." Tommie smirked and reached out between us. Her fingers were at the curve of my neck, then, drifting down, touching feather soft, until they circled the bite marks in my neck. I shuddered under that touch, the ache growing brighter beneath my skin. "But don't worry," she said, withdrawing her hand from my skin. I was breathing so quickly I was panting. "I'll help you," she said then with utter nonchalance. "If you want me to."

"That's...very nice of you," I managed, glancing back up to her eyes. They were considering me, and for a moment, I saw a flicker beneath them of something I couldn't quite place.

"I'm...very tired," I managed then, beginning to back away. I ran into Jane's table with my thigh, and she muttered something dark at me as her piles of cards for her game of solitaire shifted and merged together. "I'm sorry," I told her, and then I was across the room and out the door before I could say or do anything else.

The corridor was blessedly empty. I walked along it quickly, unhappily noting that the sun had slipped below the horizon.

Did I feel safe at the Sullivan Hotel?

Not really.

Then...why did I stay?

I didn't know. I *did* know. I...wasn't completely sure.

(Yes I was).

I practically ran the rest of the way, up the flights of stairs and down the hallways, until I reached the room of my best friend. I pounded on Gwen's door, then. She hadn't been in her room any of the recent times this last twenty-four hours that I needed her. She needed to be there now. I needed to talk to her. Not about vampires. Not *really* about vampires.

Gwen answered the door, her long, frizzy

brown hair up in a towel, and her naked body sheathed in a bathrobe, her fingers on the knob pruned. I guess I'd gotten her out of the tub. Her eyes were wide as she looked me up and down, and then she was grinning just as widely as she practically pulled me into the room.

"Why did you get so dressed up?" she practically squealed. She smelled like orange and lavender, one of her favorite bath salts. "Are you seeing someone?"

My stomach twisted in pain as I shook my head. Did I want to be seeing someone? Yes, yes I did. But...

"Anna," I whispered, then, and the joy and exuberance seemed to fade almost instantly from Gwen's face.

"I don't know what I'm doing," I told her, gripping her shoulders with tight fingers. All of the fear of what might happen in the next few days, of all the vampires who "might" not have the Sullivans' values, even my fear of Mags, took a back seat to the feeling I'd been trying to quell this entire day. And failing to. "Kane..." I trailed off as I saw the light come back to Gwen's eyes. I went to her bed, sat down on the edge of it, shoulders curved forward as I sighed. "I'm pretty attracted to her," I admitted, then, in a whisper.

"Wow," said Gwen, cinching her robe a little tighter and going to sit down on her rocking chair. It was a sweet little antique one that gave a squeak each time she rocked. "I didn't think it'd be her that you fell for," she admitted, then.

"What?" I asked, blinking. "Gwen, I shouldn't even be falling for *any* of them. Anna—"

"Died over six months ago," said Gwen gently, patiently, as she'd said a million times before. "And it's only natural that you'd be attracted to a gorgeous woman. These feelings aren't anything you should feel ashamed of, Rose," she said, leaning forward with another squeak. "I knew Anna," she whispered then, her eyes wide as she breathed out. "And she'd be furious at you if she knew how you refused to get on with your life after she was gone."

I buried my face in my hands. I was starting to forget how Anna looked when she smiled at me—just me. I was starting to forget how she smelled, the soft scent of her. In this place, I was starting to forget those beautiful little details that I wanted to impress on my memory forever. Was this right to forget them? I wasn't forgetting Anna herself, and I would *never* forget Anna. I'd loved her with everything that I was.

But...wasn't being attracted to someone betraying her?

Gwen seemed to sense my thoughts, for she got up from the rocking chair, leaving it rocking without her, and came across to sit on the bed beside me, putting a fragrant arm around my shoulder. "Honey, Anna loved you very much, and you were great together. But she's gone. You're *not*. You're alive, and you have to keep living, okay? And this is really, really great—I'm glad you're attracted to Kane. What do we think—is the feeling mutual?"

I considered Kane's smoldering gaze every time she glanced my way, the way she looked at me across a crowded room, like she could see to the deepest parts of me. But I didn't know. She was an intense, beautiful thing. Maybe she looked at everyone like that. I wasn't special.

"I don't know," I admitted. The way she'd saved me after what Mags did replayed itself in my mind, the way she glanced down at me with those perfect blue eyes...but wouldn't she have saved anyone?

What Mags did...

I shivered.

"Hey," said Gwen, then, squeezing my shoulders. "You seem a little preoccupied...and not about Anna," she said, holding up a hand when I began to protest. "Did something happen?" Concern made her brows furrow and she squeezed my shoulders again tightly. "Are you okay?"

The way she was holding so tightly to my shoulders made the now even smaller wounds on my shoulder and neck pulse with a sharp ache. I swallowed, shook my head. "No," I told her, lying to my best friend. "It's nothing. I'm fine."

"I didn't see you today at the front desk, but Kane said she'd been training you..." Gwen said, trailing off, searching my eyes, questioning. "But I didn't get any training when I was hired here."

"Well..." I said helplessly, staring down at my hands in my lap. I didn't know what else to say. I've always been a terrible liar.

"But," said Gwen, with an impish smile, changing the subject smoothly—she knew when I didn't want to talk about something, "I noticed that we're both off the schedule tomorrow. It was sweet for Kane to make certain we got a day off together. So you know what that means!"

"I couldn't possibly guess," I muttered, weak with relief that she hadn't pursued her line of questioning. Once Gwen gets it into her head that she's going to find something out, she always does. *Always.*

"We can head into town! I didn't really get to show you Eternal Cove—a drive through in the middle of the night doesn't count at all. It'll be wonderful! We can do a little shopping, get a latte—have a girl's day, all to ourselves!"

Gwen's enthusiasm was practically catching, even though—admittedly—the idea of shopping wasn't ever on my list of things I wanted to do. I hoped we'd get a chance to survey the magnificent rocky coastline of Eternal Cove—not a sales rack. "That would be really nice," I told her, then, feeling grateful that even though I was tremendously out of my depth, I still had my best friend to see me through all of this. She was so supportive, unfailingly and constantly supportive, and she'd seen me through so many other rough patches. Especially these last six months. I turned to her and hugged her tightly, and she grinned at me.

"Okay, so tomorrow morning, we're heading into town. Sound good?"

"Sure," I told her, rising and stretching. She stood, too, holding her robe closed over her heart as she considered me.

"Are you sure there's nothing else you wanted to tell me?" she pried gently. I shook my head—a little too quickly—and turned toward the door.

"I'm just tired," I told her, the wounds on my neck throbbing with a deep ache. I was so grateful I'd thought to wrap a pretty, flowing scarf around my neck, obscuring the wounds from view. If Gwen saw them, she'd never stop questioning me until she got answers...and I had no idea how I could possibly explain them. "I'm going to turn in early," I said with a tired smile.

"Okay—knock on the wall if you need

anything, okay?" She indicated the wall that stood between our rooms. I nodded and left, thoughts already a million miles away.

I promptly ran into Tommie.

"Whoa!" she grinned as the door shut behind me. She held onto my shoulders to steady me—I'd smacked into her hard—and looked down at me with a bemused grin. "Do you always assault people?" she chuckled, rubbing her jaw where my shoulder had hit her.

"I'm so sorry!" I murmured in horror, gazing up at her bright, flashing eyes, and her incredibly handsome features. Despite myself, my heart began beating a little faster.

"I just came to see if you were all right," said Tommie, one brow up. "Are you?"

All right from what? The almost-drowning this morning? The fact that the vampires I'd now realized I was living with had wanted to vote on if I could stay or not? The fact that Mags had appeared at that "meeting" seemingly just to threaten me?

"I'm fine," I lied again. Remember, I'm a terrible liar. Tommie's brows rose even higher at that, and then she was grinning at me, shaking her head a little as she shoved her hands into her pants pockets, her sharp, shoulder-length black hair seeming to curve toward me.

"I *also* came to see if you were hungry. What with the vampire blood coursing through you and all, I figured you might be." Her head was a little to the side, the brim of her fedora pushed back on her forehead so her eyes could appraise me. My breath caught as she bore the full weight of her intense gaze down on me.

"I could eat," I told her, the words hanging

between us.

"Great. There's pizza down in the kitchens," she said, tossing her head toward my room door, but not actually at my room—in the direction of the kitchens somewhere in this sprawling house, I realized.

"Oh." She stood there considering me—I hadn't realized she'd wanted to go with me (though why I didn't realize it is beyond me—I was thinking of too many other things). And I didn't want to go with her to the kitchens. The reason that moved through me so quickly I almost didn't feel its absoluteness, was that I didn't want to chance Kane seeing me with Tommie.

It was absurd. I was attracted to Tommie, but surely she wasn't attracted to me. Kane wouldn't think anything if I was with Tommie, and what if she did? I wasn't Kane's, and Kane certainly wasn't mine. I was intensely attracted to Kane, wanted to get to know her better, wanted to be merely in her presence, but that didn't mean anything.

I realized my fingernails were digging into the palms of my hands as I considered what Tommie had just said. Her eyebrows rose as I wondered what I should say in return. I waited too long.

"Hey, it was just a question—no hard feelings if you'd rather rest," she shrugged, turning smoothly on her heel as she began to stalk back down the corridor.

"No, wait!" I said, too quickly. My heart screamed "no" at me as I swallowed and nodded. "Yeah, pizza—that'd be great," I told her with a gulp and a lie. "Just let me get a sweater?"

What are you doing, *Rose? What are you doing?* It pounded like a litany in my heart as I unlocked the door to my room with my skeleton key, taking one of my favorite light brown sweaters from the little closet beside the door. The curtains in my window were open, and I saw how dark it was outside, the clouds close and not even a hint of stars in the heavens.

I wasn't *doing* anything. I was going to get food in the kitchens with someone who'd wondered if I was hungry, one of my employers. There was absolutely, positively nothing else going on. And even if I did find Tommie attractive, it wasn't like how I found Kane—this wasn't like Kane at all, what I felt for Tommie. It was simply light interest, and nothing more.

But if it was so innocent, why did I feel guilty as I exited my room, as I slipped the key into my coat pocket, and Tommie gave me an appreciative, almost wolfish grin? We walked down the hallway together, guilt making my heart beat faster.

I kept wishing that it wasn't Tommie beside me.

I kept wishing it was Kane.

"Do vampires eat pizza?" I asked her as we found our way to the spiral staircase. We began to descend.

She laughed at that, casting me a sidelong glance as she took off her fedora and ran long, graceful fingers through her short black hair before replacing the hat. "No," she admitted with a grin, "but we have other human staff members here and we like to get pizza for them on Friday nights."

So it was Friday. And that was right—I *hadn't* met the other staff members because the last two days had been a blur of vampire-related activities. I sighed and touched my fingers to the banister as we hit another landing and kept going down.

"The kitchens are actually in the basement," she told me when we reached the first floor. So we took one more curl of the stairs down. The basements themselves didn't exactly look like my vision of a basement. They were completely finished and just a little chillier than the floor above us. We walked down the tiled hallway (no longer red and black, but some pleasing Tuscan-colored gold and brown) and entered the industrial-sized kitchens. The sprawling white-walled room was well lit and looked like a cooking show could break out alongside its restaurant-quality ovens at any second. Tommie crossed to the walk-in fridge and came out with a gigantic box of pizza, about half as long as she was tall. The pizza inside was covered in foil, and she drew up two stools to the side counter as she set it out. I drew out a piece of pizza from the box, put it on a paper plate, gotten from a stack of them, and set it to re-heat in the only small appliance in the kitchen: the microwave.

As I did these actions, going through the motions, I could feel Tommie's gaze on me. When I glanced back, over my shoulder, she had her chin in her hands as she considered me with flashing green eyes.

"What?" I asked, suddenly self-conscious as I leaned against the counter.

"Nothing—you just remind me of someone I used to know," she said, her head to the side as she gazed into my face. "*Anyway*," she said, leaning back on the stool and hooking her elbows onto the counter space behind her. "There must be *something* about you," she said, her mouth twitching at the corners as she tried to suppress a smile. "Kane *did* want you to stay."

At that, the butterflies I'd been trying to quell in my heart began to flutter against the insides of my ribs again, pushing, poking and prodding with feather-soft wings of hopefulness. "Why…why do you say that?" I asked, licking my lips and trying to appear nonchalant. I failed at that as she chuckled at me, shaking her head, her hair swishing around her chin as she narrowed her eyes.

"She *said* she wanted you to stay," said Tommie, one brow up. Her grin widened, then, as the microwave beeped, startling me. "Say...do you have a thing for our fearless leader?" The last two words didn't exactly sound like a compliment as she practically snarled them out. I paused at that, but opened the microwave door and took out my tasty conquest, blowing on the piece of pizza that made the paper plate bow out in the middle. I set it down beside Tommie and perched on the edge of the stool.

I wasn't used to telling people my problems or my past, but I *had* just found out that Tommie was a vampire, so I figured it might be best to, in this at least, be truthful. And, perhaps convince myself that I didn't actually have feelings for Kane. "I...I don't," I lied, swallowing. "It's because...I mean, I'm still dealing with the fact that I lost my girlfriend six months ago," I told her, chewing on my lip a little as I glanced down at the plate. "To a drunk driver."

"Huh," is what Tommie said, and when I glanced back up at her, she didn't have the patented, sympathetic, brows furrowed and frown that most people adopt when you tell them that your partner was killed. It seemed like she hadn't even heard me. She was looking at me a little...hungrily.

I stared at her with wide eyes, and she blinked, seemed to realize she'd been staring. She shook her head a little.

"Well," she said a little bitterly, pushing up her hat again as she sighed and leaned a little harder against the counter with a grimace, "I guess that would make two of you then. Kane lost her partner, too."

"What?" I asked, suddenly going cold. Why did I have ridiculous, intense and painful jealousy that, all of a sudden, seemed to be consuming me? It was too quick and sharp and far too potent. I swallowed, clenching a fist under the table as I stared down at my soggy pizza.

"Her name was Melody," said Tommie, drawing out the name with a languorous tone as I stared at her. Another shiver moved through me. She glanced sidelong at me with a frown. "She was...she was beautiful, I'll give you that. There was something about her, about her smile. It unnerved you, I guess, how good she was—she'd go out of her way to help you. Once, she helped me..." Tommie shook her head, glancing my way, her tone—all at once softening— turned hard and malicious again. "It was just all this unbelievable soul mate romantic crap between the two of them, Kane and Melody. They were inseparable— were desperately in love. True love, they both said. Kane loved her a bit too much, if you ask me—it was practically obsessive," she muttered glancing at the overhead fluorescent bulbs with narrowed eyes. "So they were incredibly in love, but they still lost each other. Kane lost her a long time ago, a tragic death. So, since then, Kane hasn't dated or, hell, *slept* with anyone since in memory of her, like some twisted, tragic loyalty. Isn't that ridiculous? It's just...it's *sick*." She glanced back down at me, her mouth turning up at the corners again as she laughed at it. "That kind of stuff should be put in books and stay there. It's not *realistic*. Kane loved the woman, okay. Whatever. But after she loses her, turning into a chaste puritan or some shit in her memory? I don't get it. While I'm here, I'm going to enjoy life's little pleasures." She looked pointedly at the plunge in my dress that my sweater wasn't exactly covering. I pushed my half-eaten piece of pizza away, drew my sweater more closed over my chest. I'd suddenly lost my appetite.

My heart felt like it was breaking.

So no. That meant that Kane didn't feel anything between us. How could she? She was still remembering her soul mate love…her true love in Melody, the woman she'd lost a long time ago. She was staying true to her, even after all this time, and how could I possibly begrudge her that? Couldn't I, with how I'd mourned Anna, understand that much?

Yes, I know that I'd hoped that what I was seeing from her were signals, some sort of sign that there was interest there, in her toward me. But I'd misread everything—I'd been, in fact, completely wrong.

The space where my heart resides began to actually hurt, a deep, piercing ache that pained me much more than the healing wounds in my neck. I breathed out, trying to quell the rising pain, the deep and profound sadness that wanted to fill me completely, when I heard, far distant, a gong that sounded a little like chimes or bells. It reminded me of a front door bell.

Tommie raised her head, and smoothly stood, kicking the stool back under the counter with one shiny shoe and shoving her hands deeply into pants pockets, hunching her shoulders forward. "I'll talk to you later, yeah? That's the first guest." As she moved past me, her hipbone grazed my side perhaps unintentionally, but my heart beat a little faster, my body responding to a signal when my head and heart weren't remotely involved. She turned to toss me a smirk and a wink over her shoulder, but she kept walking. She left the kitchens, and I was alone with my sadness.

Funny how a single piece of knowledge can make or break you. I shouldn't have been so utterly consumed by Kane Sullivan, but the feelings that I had for that completely unexpected woman in my life, that vampire, weren't something that I could have predicted, and it certainly wasn't something I could control or quell, even if I'd wanted to. And now I knew she could not or would not be mine. When had it happened, her love affair with Melody? How long is a "long time ago?" Centuries? A century? Decades? Since then, Kane Sullivan had probably seen thousands of beautiful women, much prettier than me, more attractive, more beguiling, and had withstood all of them, if she'd ever even wanted anyone after losing Melody. Just because my heart beat faster when she was around, just because I was drawn to her utterly meant nothing. I wanted her. She did not want me.

I wanted her.

I stood, picking up the greasy paper plate and the half-eaten slice of pizza and deposited them into the shiny revolving trashcan's mouth. I put the pizza box back into the walk-in fridge, and I stood for a moment in the too-bright kitchens, rubbing at my arms with cold hands, my body curving toward the door.

I felt lost.

Tears pricked my eyes, but I wouldn't let them spill. Angrily, I dashed them away with my sweater's sleeve as I glanced around, realizing there was no reason for me to stay down here, in the kitchens. I'd lost my appetite and my hope for Kane, all in the space of five minutes. I'd find my way back to my rooms from here—you just keep heading ever upward, right? I could get there.

But I didn't really feel at that moment, in my life, that I was remotely headed upward.

I felt stupid, shame coursing through me that I'd ever even carried a hope for Kane Sullivan. How could I be so naive? But when I closed my eyes, I saw that perfect curve of her pale jaw, the slope of her neck, the full lips and the brilliant blue eyes that pinned me in place, that made and remade me as I was consumed by them. I wanted to feel the silky strands of her hair as they draped around me, I wanted to feel the cool press of her lips against my mouth as she leaned over me, her shadow covering my body, her hands against my...

I gasped, my breath catching in my throat as I stood, shaking beneath those too-bright fluorescent lights. Oh, how I ached. What was wrong with me? Why did it hurt this much, this knowledge that Kane and I would never be?

I didn't understand it. I crossed to the far side of the room, flicked all the lights off, one by one down the row on the metal plate as I dashed away more tears from my watery eyes, and I began to walk down the corridor in the basement, my flats clicking against the tiles like my too-fast heartbeat.

Above me, I could hear muffled, distant voices.

I traveled up the spiral staircase, and because I felt guilt at not remotely having done my job that day, I didn't go back up to my room. I hoped that I wasn't too flushed from my tears, but other than that, I was presentable and whoever was currently manning the front desk probably needed some help if there were a lot of guests to check in. So I walked down the hallway of paintings quickly, resolved, the red and black checkered tiles moving swiftly under my feet. I wanted to be helpful. What the hell were they paying me for if I wasn't?

I paused, though, when I rounded the final corner past a painting of a man, sitting alone on a violet and gold mountain. How fitting—it's how I currently wanted to be to deal with my pain. But I wouldn't get the chance. Because there was a line of people and suitcases and trunks stretching out the front door.

And Kane, and only Kane, was behind the big, wooden front desk.

"The usual, Eleanor?" came her cool, smooth voice, rolling across the space between us to wash over me. When she spoke, my body responded, and I didn't understand it, and I didn't like it. Not even Anna had held that much power over me, but when I heard Kane's tongue and lips form syllables, my heart skipped beats, and I was tugged closer to her, like she held a rope around my heart and was squeezing, pulling, drawing me in.

As if she felt the weight of my gaze on her, Kane straightened, rolling up one of her dress shirt sleeves (her suit's jacket lying on the stool behind her) a little higher and glanced in my direction. Her bright blue eyes widened almost imperceptibly when she saw me, but she said nothing, only handed the woman before her—a stunning creature with pumps that made her practically walk on her tiptoes, and covered in an appalling fur coat—an old-fashioned silver skeleton key.

I made my way across the distance, sliding behind the wide expanse of the oaken front desk, turning to Kane as she pushed the guest book gently across the desktop toward the next guest, a tall man with piercing brown eyes and a delicately curled mustache dressed in a smart tweed suit.

"Do you need help?" I asked her, and Kane then cast a sidelong glance at me, appraising me. The corners of her mouth, to my delight, curled upward, and she was nodding a little, handing the man an expensive looking fountain pen.

"If you would give Reginald the key for 313, that would be lovely," she said, voice a rumble as she nodded to him, the man scratching his name down into the book.

I turned to the wall behind the both of us, covered in pegs and keys on leather key rings like you might have seen a hundred years ago at the best hotels. I chose the one beneath the small metal plate, corroded with rust, that read "313" and handed it across the wide front desk to the man who exchanged the key with me for the pen.

The woman after Reginald had such pale skin it was almost translucent. Her face looked young, but there was an air about her of age and timelessness. Her long, curling inky-black hair almost fell down to the backs of her legs as she stepped forward gingerly, her midnight blue gown flaring out around her knees. It hung off her painfully thin shoulders like it'd been sewn for a different woman. She gazed at me with milky blue eyes as she tilted her head slowly. I shivered.

"Who's that?" she asked Kane, her soft voice high-pitched as Kane handed her the pen and pushed the guest book gently in front of her.

"This is Rose, Maggie," said Kane softly, her gaze not on the old woman, but on me. "She just arrived to help at the Sullivan Hotel—she's a new hire here, you've not met her before."

"Rose?" asked the woman, persisting, as if she disbelieved Kane. She reached across the table, and I held out the key that Kane had pressed into my hands with her cold fingers, but it didn't seem like the key had been what Maggie was after. Instead, she curled her bony fingers into my palm, groping my hand, as if she was searching for something.

"Kane, how foolish—this isn't Rose," said Maggie seriously, but Kane shook her head, handing the pen to the next guest in line.

"I'm Rose," I told this strange woman gently, but then her fingers were pricking my skin, her fingernails sharp and pin-like against me, more painful than they should have been, and her young-looking nose sniffed the air. She unnerved me.

"Maggie, here's your key," said Kane firmly, taking my hand in her right as she pushed the key forward with her left. And the woman took up that key, then, holding it over her heart as she cocked her head at me and looked at me with those milky blue eyes. She could see out of them, it seemed, because she followed me with her gaze as I stepped backward, but it seemed that she was looking past me, too.

After a long, awkward moment, she curled her claw-like fingers around the key and turned, walking down the gallery of paintings with an uneven step, her back to me.

There were some in this first wave of guests who definitely struck me as vampires (like Maggie), but there were just as many who looked like they were on a business trip and were going to ask me if their room had Wifi and what sort of gym and other amenities we had at this hotel. There were men and women who looked nothing like what I had ever assumed vampires to be—they didn't even appear pale, which I suppose is a cliché, but most of the Sullivans were pale (though, admittedly, not all of them).

I was just doing my best to uncover everything I could about what made a vampire...a vampire. And those answers didn't appear as easily as I would have hoped.

After we'd checked everyone in, Kane sighed, closing the guest book for the night, and plucked up her jacket from the stool, shrugging into it with one graceful motion.

"That's the first wave of them," she said then, her voice soft and deep. I turned to her as I slid the pen into its little wooden box beneath the counter. "For the Conference," she said, adjusting her jacket's collar and tightening her tie, straightening it with long, slender fingers. "Did anyone tell you about it?"

"Um, a little," I said, fingering the fringed edge of my sweater. "Vampires, from all over the world, come together for a...meeting?"

She chuckled at that, a sound that caused a (hopefully) imperceptible shudder of pleasure to move through me. "That's...an interesting description. That's a little of what the Conference is, but there's more to it then that. The vampires of the world must meet to discuss many things. You'll get to see bits and pieces of it, be involved in it a little—and there's a dance at the very end of it..." She gazed at me quietly, her blue eyes constant and piercing.

We stood there then, just the two of us in the now-quiet entrance. My body curved toward her like an arrow, something I couldn't control, just like I couldn't control what I wanted or how much my heart hurt looking at her.

I knew what I wanted. And it wasn't something I could possibly have.

"Do you always walk late a night?" Kane asked the surprising question, then, her head to the side as she considered me, her long, white-blonde hair pooling over her shoulder. I breathed in, paling.

"How did you know that?" I asked her.

She shrugged a little, adjusting her sleeves beneath the jacket, tugging them out. "It was just an odd hour for a walk this morning. I wondered if you often do it." She seemed to be searching my face.

"Yes. I love to walk at night," I breathed.

She didn't look at me as she stepped forward, her gaze was down, the intensity of her blue eyes muted by her long, blonde lashes. She was close enough that I could inhale the scent of her, that delicious vanilla mingling with the rich, warm aroma of jasmine that caused a tightening in my chest. She shifted her gaze, and she did look down at me then, her blue eyes darkening as she gazed into me.

What was this then, if not attraction? I wanted to ask her, ask her if my heart beating so quickly was answered by her own. How fast can a vampire's heart beat? I wished deeply and darkly that it mirrored mine. My breath came fast and as she stood so close to me, her scent engulfing me with a want and a need that my body, my head and my heart were in complete and unanimous agreement on. She straightened then, her face suddenly becoming impassive as she turned away from me, walked past me and out from behind the front desk.

"I enjoy walking at night, too," she told me, her back to me as she pulled her ponytail over her shoulder

133

and straightened it. The brightly-glittering hair lying in her hands like a pool of satin caused my breath to come shorter. I wanted to touch those perfect strands, run my fingers through them, take out her ponytail and watch the length and shimmer of her hair fall around her perfect shoulders. She turned to me, her eyes searching mine as her head inclined toward the door. "Would you like to go for a walk with me?" she asked then. Her words were soft and low, but in that stillness, they seemed to be projected clearly into my heart.

"Yes," I was saying before I'd even processed the question, was already out from behind the front desk, too, already alongside her before my brain caught up with the question asked. The right corner of her mouth curved up a little at that, and she inclined her head to me in something that was almost akin to a little bow as she offered her arm to me once more.

I slid my arm into hers like it was meant to be there, my fingers brushing against the cool softness of her suit jacket's sleeve.

We crossed the space of the entrance together, and her hand was on the scrolled silver of the doorknob before she turned to me, one brow up.

"You're only wearing a sweater—won't you be cold?" she asked me.

"No," I told her, which wasn't a very convincing lie, but she shook her head with a small, throaty chuckle, and then the door was open, and we were out beneath the stars.

The cloud cover from earlier seemed to have lifted, for the heavens were spangled above us, brilliant and bright with the milky way arching overhead, pointing, it seemed, ever onward and downward, toward the sea.

"Sometimes," she whispered into my ear, the coolness of her breath making me shiver against her, "you can see the aurora borealis from here. A thousand colors, all drifting together like a great dance."

Her words washed over me, and I felt my heart lift as we stood together between the front columns of the Sullivan Hotel, the both of us looking up at that beautiful night sky, beautiful even without the sight of the aurora borealis. I could imagine those colors, as her syllables entered me, but most of all, I could imagine watching it with her.

We took the steps and began walking across the gravel, our shoes crunching against it, toward the path that led down to the sea. I should have been unhappy to go back there—I did almost die there that morning—but I felt nothing more than giddy happiness (and, admittedly, a bit of cold) to be out here in the night with Kane and Kane alone.

I tried not to think about what Tommie had just told me. That Kane had not dated anyone since her partner had passed away, a very, very long time ago. I was here with her right now, wasn't I? And this was perfectly innocent, I knew, strolling down a path with her, arm in arm. Kane was old fashioned, and offering her arm to me meant absolutely nothing. I *knew* that. But just for a few moments with her by my side, I could pretend. I could pretend that this was so much more than taking a late night stroll together, content in one another's companionship.

I wasn't content. It had come quickly and fiercely upon me, this want and need, something I hadn't felt for so long. And it frightened me, how much I wanted her to look at me with want, too. I ached for that, the ache stronger than the wounds far above my heart, the wounds that ached dully in my neck. But wasn't it enough to just be with her?

I felt, when I was with Kane Sullivan, that all of the pain of my life was somehow lessened. All of the scars on my heart, all of the moments I'd suffered, were somehow made better. That's the only way I can think to describe it. That, by being around her, the good of the world was confirmed, the miraculous and the beautiful were made clear, and I could suddenly see how lovely life was, how precious each day was, how important and beautiful a single moment could be. I turned to her, then, as we continued in our way down the smoothly sloping path, down to the sand and the beach. The starlight was reflected in her bright blue eyes, and they seemed to glow with that light of the stars. Her gaze was downcast, looking down at the beach, at the pulsing rhythm of the waves, but her eyes seemed a million miles away.

That is, until we reached the sand.

Kane turned to me, then, those bright blue eyes, still so bright, even in the darkness, seemed to be searching my face. "I'm sorry about what Mags did to you," she whispered, then, her deep, dark voice so soft, so gentle, that I shivered as she stared deeply into me. It felt like her voice was caressing me, the satin feel of the words drifting over my skin as I tilted my head up, as she tilted her head down. She was standing so close to me, because she'd not yet let go of my arm. I didn't want her to. I held tightly to it, because at least, for this moment, we were this close.

But she stepped closer still.

"I want you to know, Rose, that I will make certain it never happens again. I...I don't want you to fear being here. I want you to know that you are, and will always be, safe at the Sullivan Hotel." She searched my eyes, first one, then the other, her breath coming faster as she took her other hand and gathered my fingers in its palm. Her skin was so cold, and I shivered beneath that soft touch, as much as I shivered beneath her gaze, her words.

Silently, Kane let go of me, then. She let go, and she took off her suit jacket. Like she was in an old black and white movie, Kane slipped the smooth material around my shoulders, tugging a little at the collar to straighten it.

Her hands remained curled against the collar.

Over my heart.

"I'll keep you safe," she whispered.

I gazed up into her eyes, her eyes that reflected the stars back to me so clearly. My heart beat too fast, my breath came too fast, but still, I parted my lips, I opened my mouth. I had to know. I couldn't keep the question from being asked, so I simply spoke it:

"Why?"

Her brow furrowed at that, and her head went to the side a little as she gazed down at me.

"Why do you want to keep me safe?" I asked, blood roaring in my ears, a blush crawling over my skin as I began to wonder if I'd misread everything. Tommie was right. There was nothing that Kane felt for me other than what an employer feels for her employee. Every employer wants to make certain their employee works in a safe environment, don't they? I felt so stupid as I stood there beneath her gaze, tears pricking at the corners of my eyes as I blinked them back, as I began to lean away from her.

The ache inside of me grew too tremendous for me to bear.

But then, Kane shook her head. She stepped forward again, and then her hands over my heart were caught between us as she pressed the length of her body against mine. She was hard, her stomach, her legs, and she was so soft, her breasts, her gaze, as she stared down into me, into every place of me, seeing me wholly and completely as she breathed out, as the sweet scent of all that was Kane Sullivan washed over me, and my body responded to it, leaning toward her, drawn toward her.

"Rose," she whispered, and a shiver ran through me that this perfect mouth had said my name, the syllable a deep rumble that moved through her into a softness as she gazed down at me. "I want to keep you safe," she said softly, quietly, each word perfect and clear like the starlight above us, "because I am compelled to."

"Why?" I whispered, every inch of my skin hot, my heart growing within me.

"Because..." She searched my face carefully, as if she was memorizing every curve of my skin, because, in that moment, I was memorizing hers. "From the very first moment I met you, touched you, there has been something in me that is answered by you," she whispered as I began to shake against her. "I am compelled by you and your presence, I am drawn to your voice, your shape, everything about you the very essence of one I know completely. But I've never met you," she breathed, searching my face as I stood up on my tiptoes as I softly, tentatively wrapped my arms around her waist. It was an unconscious motion, but suddenly my arms were there and they felt so right on those perfect curves that I ached for touching her, ached deep within my body, a pleasant, delicious ache that seemed to spread through the whole of me.

"There is something in you, Rose," she whispered, "something that calls to me." She turned her face slightly, and she bowed her beautiful neck, but she did not kiss my mouth. She pressed her lips to the skin of my neck, and I shivered under the cool softness of them, shivered as I arched my head back, exposing more of my skin to her as her mouth opened, and she pressed one sweet, salty kiss to my skin. "It calls me gently." Another kiss. Lower. I breathed out, closed my eyes, felt the press of her body against me, my arms gripping around her arms now as she pressed her open mouth against the skin of the space at the base of my neck, where it meets my chest, that small triangle there. "It calls me strongly," she whispered, and then she was straightening, her hands at the base of my neck, pulling me forward, and another strongly and tightly at my hips as she guided her own against mine. "You call me, Rose," she said.

She kissed me, then.

Her mouth was soft and cold and warm, all at once, and it was open against me, her lips against mine, breathing me in as she kissed me gently at first. But I wrapped my own arms around her neck, and I drew her down to me, pulled tight and strong against me as she bent her beautiful head and kissed me deeply. She tasted cold and sweet, like peppermint, but there was an unfamiliar taste to her, too, something metallic and almost too-sweet, but I hardly noticed as she pressed against me, as her mouth grew bolder, asking more. I opened up to her as she pressed her chill fingers against my neck, causing a shudder to move through me, a shudder I couldn't quell.

The jacket fell from my shoulders, fell with a

shush against the sand as we became wrapped in one another's arms. I wanted her with such a sudden and intense ferocity, I was consumed by it. But I didn't want to press her, push her. Tommie had told me that Kane had lost her partner...how long ago? Maybe decades or only a few years, but maybe it had happened hundreds of years ago. I didn't know how long, but that she was changing how she approached the world for me was a precious thing I wanted and needed to honor. I craved her in such completeness that I almost wept from how much I wanted her, how much I felt for her. Was this possible? It had only been a few days, but somehow, impossibly, I had found myself falling for Kane so quickly and utterly that there was no part of me that was not wholly consumed by her. She consumed me like fire, and nothing of what I had once been remained.

I felt remade by her.

I felt undone by her.

Her hand behind my neck crept to the edge of my dress's top as she kissed me, a delicate thumb pressing under the material at the neck to the skin there. I breathed out against her as she pressed her thumb's pad to me, how searing cool it was, but I was so hot beneath her that the cold and hot seemed to merge, somehow. I leaned against her, breathing out.

And against me, Kane stiffened.

She pulled back from me, her breath coming quickly, in short gasps, as she gazed questioningly down at me.

"What is it?" I whispered, trying to keep my voice calm, quiet. It echoed around us, melting with the *shush* of the waves, far down the beach.

"I heard...something," said Kane, then,

carefully, glancing back up the path we'd come down. There was nothing there, only the low angle of the path, and—far above us, on the cliff—the shrubs that had been planted there who knew how long ago.

She glanced down at me again, and her eyes were dark, so dark with longing that all I was responded to it. She wrapped me in her arms, and she bent her head to drink me in again...

But she paused.

We both turned. And I knew that we had both seen it.

Coming down the path toward us was the lone figure of a woman. She walked slowly, carefully, as if she didn't know the way, her hair streaming out behind her in the starlight could have been any color, but it was full and curly and wavy and she wore a dress that flowed out behind her, too. Though the night was very cold, she wore no coat or sweater, only a dress that had no sleeves, of a gauzy material that would be better worn in a painting than in real life.

But as she came toward us, a strong, bad feeling began to unfurl in my stomach. Kane stared at this woman as she came closer, as her features became more distinguished, and then the unthinkable happened.

Kane stepped away from me. She stepped away from me, and she stood there, in the dark, as the woman paused at the very edge of the path, her bare feet an inch from the sand.

There was something so strange about her. So familiar. I stared at her, at her long hair that somehow, impossibly, I knew was red, at the upturned nose and the smiling mouth and the curvaceous body.

She held out a single hand. And it was not to me.

Kane took one step forward, her mouth open, her bright blue eyes filling with tears.

She whispered one word, and it was that single word that broke my world apart:

"...Melody?"

-- Eternal Thief --

Kane stood squarely on the sand, staring up at this impossible ghost from her past, this beautiful woman who stood above her on the path. My mouth was still warm, still wet from our kiss, and my whole body was *alive* from that kiss...

But it seemed, as Kane stared at this woman, that Kane didn't even know I was here anymore.

Standing above her, on the path down to the sea, stood a beautiful creature that I shouldn't have recognized—but did. She had long, flowing red hair, and she wore a gauzy, flimsy dress that was almost suicidal on this chill October night, with the ocean crashing away behind us, its frothing waves pounding against the unrelenting sand. But as the chill wind blew, stirring the sea grasses and blowing our hair about our shoulders, it seemed that this stranger didn't seem to care about the cold, about her dress, about anything really—except for Kane.

She held one pretty hand out to Kane, palm up, long lovely fingers extended toward her, curling slightly as if she beckoned Kane forward, and Kane who watched this woman move with haunted eyes opened her beautiful, full lips and repeated the word, the word that destroyed me:

"Melody?" Kane's voice, usually so smoky and smooth and low came out anguished, pained, as she stood there with her legs apart, her hands curled into fists. Though she stood with her usual graceful strength, though she leaned forward powerfully, she was shaking a little, I realized, in shock. Kane *looked* like she saw a ghost, but the woman before us was too substantial to be anything other than real. She wasn't transparent.

She was...*real*.

And if this was Melody, the Melody who Tommie told me about only that afternoon, then it meant this was the Melody who Kane had loved with all of her heart, the Melody who had supposedly died, though I don't know how long ago. The Melody who Kane had sworn was her true love and soul mate, what Tommie had called "romantic garbage."

But Melody was dead, or—at least—she was supposed to be, had been, and though Tommie hadn't told me how long ago it happened, she seemed to imply that it had been at least decades, if not longer, since Melody had last walked the earth. And though Kane had, since Melody's death, not even looked at another woman, when I'd arrived at the Sullivan Hotel...well. We both started looking at each other.

And Kane had *just* told me, mere moments before, that she's begun falling in love with me. And I'd been falling in love with her, something I could finally admit to myself now—but it didn't matter, because now my entire world of possibilities was shattered by this beautiful stranger walking down the path to the beach, a sure smile on her lips as she held both of her hands out to Kane.

She strode toward Kane without a care in the world, to take back what had only been hers.

What had never been mine.

A single tear fell down Kane's cheek from her too-blue eyes, eyes that were so often violently blue, icy blue, housing the deep power that thrummed through Kane, the power that had first attracted me to her. But there was nothing but sadness, but confusion on her handsome face now as she stared up at Melody walking down the path toward us, as that one tear seemed to catch all of the starlight in the sky as it fell slowly over Kane's perfect, pale skin.

Melody took the last step down from the path, and she was finally standing on the sand of the beach itself. She was about a head shorter than Kane, but height didn't seem to matter, since power seemed to radiate from her like heat as she took one last lazy step forward to stand right in front of Kane. She lifted her pale arms around Kane's waist, and then she was drawing Kane closer. Kane caved to her, pressing herself against Melody's body, then, as she put her long-fingered hands against Melody's face, cupping her fine cheeks in her palms, peering down into her eyes, searching them for some sort of answer.

"But...how?" Kane whispered, searching her face, her own contorted with anguish. "You were *dead*." The word came out broken.

Melody gazed up at her adoringly as my stomach turned, as she shook her head, the red waves of her hair shifting lightly. "We have a lot of catching up to do," she promised, her voice as soft as a purr, and then one of her hands was at the back of Kane's neck, and she drew Kane down to her.

And kissed her.

Revulsion roared up through me, though I should have felt nothing but happiness for them. Melody, the love of Kane's life, her *soul mate*, had supposedly been dead. And now...she obviously wasn't, because she stood there, pressed against Kane so tightly that there was not a molecule of space between their bodies as their mouths merged together. And it was wonderful for Kane to have her back. I loved Kane--I wanted her to be happy with all of my heart. I should feel happy for her, should be joyful for her.

But I couldn't be.

And as I watched (I couldn't tear my eyes away--I know I should have given them a private moment, but I couldn't...too much feeling roared through me), Melody's eyes flicked open, her long black lashes fluttering against her too-pale face. She was positioned in such a way that she could just peer at me over Kane's shoulder.

And she did. As she kissed Kane, the woman I had, not a moment earlier, kissed myself, drinking her in as one of the best, gentlest and most beautiful experiences of my life, this new woman now, this new woman who was destroying anything I might have ever had with Kane, *stared* at me.

Her eyes flashed and narrowed in the darkness as if she was laughing at me. She looked, in that moment, smug and confidant.

But there was something else there, something deeper. My stomach turned as she stared at me over Kane's shoulder, eyes wide in the darkness.

There was something...wrong there. Something deep inside her that I only saw a shadow of. But it was enough.

I couldn't watch anymore. I reached up, brushed my fingers over my own lips, still swollen from the passionate kiss Kane and I had just shared, and I felt a great sob begin to rise in me. I couldn't be there anymore. I couldn't see this. I was too upset to think clearly—how many people have *just* had their first wonderful kiss with a woman they think could be *the one*, and then any possibility of that gets snatched away almost immediately after? Probably a very, very small number in the whole history of the world.

And here I was, lucky enough to be one of them.

I choked down my small sob, leaving Kane's suit jacket—the one she'd so generously and chivalrously put about my shoulders only a few short moments before—crumpled on the sand, like all my hopes, and I moved past Melody and Kane, Kane who was too wrapped up in the embrace and kiss to even notice I was leaving.

I ran the rest of the way up the path. I didn't look back once. When I was far enough away that I thought they wouldn't hear, I let out my breath in a great, rushing sob, pressing my hand against the side of the cliff face, almost doubled over with grief.

It felt like my heart was being squeezed. "Breaking" wasn't the appropriate word, really.

It felt more like my heart was being destroyed.

I wished terrible things in that moment. I wished I'd never come to the Sullivan Hotel. I wished I'd never left my plain, boring life in New Hampshire, the life where nothing exciting ever happened to me, where I could continue to live in the same apartment I'd lived in with my now dead girlfriend, keeping everything from when we were together, from when she was *alive,* constant so that I could never, ever, ever get hurt. I wished, in short, that I'd never *tried.*

It's because I came to Maine that this happened.

It's because I tried new things that this happened. It's because I'd tried to be brave, build a new and different life for myself, that this happened.

I ran across the gravel parking lot, the sprawling red stone walls of the Sullivan Hotel towering overhead seemed to leer toward me, utterly foreboding and not the least bit welcoming. I'd thought this big red stone house was going to be my new home, full of possibility.

And all it had brought me was sadness.

I pushed open the front door, and there, in the large waiting area of the hotel, sat a woman I'd never seen before, lounging on one of the antique velvet-covered couches in the waiting area before the front desk. She wore a short black pencil skirt and cream-colored blouse, and her dark blonde hair was swept up in a messy updo. She looked like she should be behind a desk in a mahogany-colored office, but instead she was sprawled on the couch, the first few buttons on her blouse undone...and there was Tommie, practically straddling her.

Drinking from two tiny wounds in her neck.

Tommie's fangs, exactly like when Kane had given me blood back in order to save me, were elongated and lengthened, and her tongue made little wet sounds as she suckled at the wounds, her eyes almost rolling back in her head as her hands squeezed the woman's breasts like they were on a bed somewhere hidden away, instead of in an entrance to a hotel.

Unlike when Mags lured me out to try to drown and drink me dry in the ocean, this seemed like a consensual sort of thing, though it still turned my stomach as I watched the pretty woman writhe beneath Tommie's administrations, the blood seeming so red beneath the hotel's lights. Tommie's chin-length black hair was being held in the woman's pink-nailed hands, and Tommie's fedora was on the other side of the couch, as if it'd been tossed off in a hurry.

I walked past them quickly. But even though Tommie was...occupied, she still noticed.

"Rose?" She slurred the word as if she was about five or six beers in to the night. I wondered if drinking blood did something for vampires, then realized that was probably a silly question. Of course it probably did something for them, probably made them feel drunk or who-knew-what-else, or why would they ever do it if they didn't have a reason to? I still had a lot to learn about vampires.

No.

Maybe I had nothing more to learn about vampires.

Maybe I'd leave.

I walked quickly down the hallway, ignoring Tommie's calls of my name, but then she was trotting after me, buttoning up the last few buttons of her spotless white shirt, adjusting her plum-colored tie so that it was straight, and plunking her much-abused fedora on her head. She was a very clean drinker, it seemed. Her lips were a little redder than usual, and her incisors were descended, but other than that, there wasn't a speck of blood on her.

"Hey," she said, all but dancing in front of me, holding out her hands, her brows furrowed as she frowned down at me. "What the hell's the matter?"

"What do you care?" It was a petulant, childish reaction, but I was too upset and too tired to be speaking to anyone right now. I wanted her to go back to that pretty woman and keep drinking and to leave me the hell alone.

"Rose, what's the *matter*?" she repeated, stepping forward, her strong hands closing around my upper arms. I stood there, then, her skin radiating heat through my sweater. Maybe it's because she'd just fed that she was warm, I thought dully in the back of my mind. Usually, vampire skin was freezing.

And why *did* she care?

"I thought you said Melody was dead," I told her, then. It came out a little dazed, and when I'd said the words, I looked at Tommie's face.

She let go of me. She stepped back as if struck.

She, too, looked like she saw a ghost.

"Rose, what do you mean?" she whispered, her eyes wide. Around us, the hall of paintings stretched on with the little lamps over the frame of each, showcasing the piece of artwork, the only light in the hall, the red and black tile floor beneath our feet seeming to devour that sparse light.

"Good night," I muttered, moving past her. I didn't know what else to say. I was sure Kane was going to use the front door when she and Melody were done on the beach (done with what? Oh, I was just hurting myself now to think of Kane's hands on Melody's body, to think of Kane's mouth…no, no, no, I had to stop thinking about that), and then if Tommie kept playing with that woman back on the couch, she'd see exactly what I'd been talking about.

I thought for a moment that Tommie was going to follow me, press me for answers. But she, mercifully, didn't. I walked quickly to the far spiral staircase, and I ascended the steps until I reached my floor, and then I ran the rest of the way to my door, fumbling with my skeleton key at the lock.

It was very late when I finally entered my

bedroom. I collapsed on my bed. I didn't even take off my sweater or my shoes. I pillowed my head in my arms, curled up my body like it was under attack, curling tightly in the fetal position, and there was no sobs, no sound, as the tears leaked quietly from my eyes, falling soundlessly to the coverlet beneath my arm.

Every time I closed my eyes, I saw Melody and Kane together, kissing, embracing, Melody's eyes open and wide and staring at me with the exact same expression I thought a wolf must wear when it closes in for the kill. I didn't want to replay that moment over and over, so I tried to stare at my pretty turquoise walls, tried to keep my eyes open, tried to think of nothing.

But I must have closed my eyes eventually, because I fell into a deep, dark sleep.

Somewhere, in the back of my head, I knew I was dreaming.

Because Kane was kissing me again.

Melody wasn't there. Perhaps she'd never come. I could hear the ocean behind us, but it sounded…different, the sibilant hiss as it pounded against the shore taking on a different cadence then what I was now used to on that stretch of Maine coastline. Even the stars overhead, where the constellations had swung low, toward the water, were also different, as if it was a different time of year. But I wouldn't know what the sky looked like there at any other time of year because I'd only been at the Sullivan Hotel a few days, had never experienced it in other seasons.

But still, the stars were different. And it was

strange.

    Kane backed away from our warm, passionate kiss—I could feel my heartbeat strongly in my lips, surging through me, the softness of her mouth, the warmth and brightness of her body against mine, how sharply I noticed each sensation, her breasts pressing against me, the angle of her hips hard against mine. She backed away, and she looked down at me with those bright, icy blue eyes with a deep longing that moved through me, captivating me, pinning me in place.

    She wore different clothes, older clothes, I suppose. It looked like she was dressed up for a costume party in her long velvet coat (I couldn't tell the color in the dark) with the lace-edged sleeves, the high collar and the plunging neckline. But draped over the collar and against her cream-colored neck was a looping black necklace, all shiny black beads and bright silver chain that flashed in the starlight. My eyes were drawn to that, to the rise in her chest, and she laughed a little, a low, growling sound that made my skin rise with goosebumps, made me shiver as I stared up at her, then.

    We were no longer on the beach. Or perhaps we'd never been there, and I'd imagined everything else. For now we stood on red and black tile in a large, impressive-looking room complete with chandeliers covered thickly with guttering tapers and candelabras and floor to ceiling length mirrors, and women and men in long gowns and long coats, danced together to a piece of music that was vaguely familiar and classical.

    Outside of one of the tall windows, the stars continued to burn as Kane took my hand with her icy fingers, began to lead me in the dance.

    We passed a mirror, and as I glanced at my

reflection, I began to feel cold.

It wasn't *me* in the mirror.

I breathed out, eyes open in an instant, but as I panted in and out, trying to calm my racing heart, bits and pieces of the dream began to disintegrate. The harder I tried to hold on to them, to remember them, the faster my impressions of the dream disappeared.

I lay there for a very long moment, aware that there was sunshine pooling warmly on the floor, that it was morning. I closed my eyes and listened to the sounds of the house waking up. Somewhere on this floor, someone was playing a classic rock station, and I could hear a much-muted guitar riff. There was the clank of pipes and the white-noise of running water rushing through the old walls. They were all good, comforting sounds, and as I stretched in bed, I brushed a finger against my lips.

And then I remembered Kane. I blushed as I lay there, remembering our kiss, remembering her cool mouth against mine, how I'd felt, in that moment, so completed, so undone by her. She'd told me before she'd kissed me that I compelled her, that she was drawn to me.

I was so purely happy in that moment. All of my feelings for Kane...she'd felt them, *too*.

And then everything else from last night came rushing back. And I remembered that I had nothing to be happy about at all.

Because somehow, impossibly, Melody had returned. And she had taken Kane from me.

It wasn't true, though. I had to be honest with

myself. Melody had, of course, come long before me. Kane was hers, had always been hers. She had never been mine.

But true or not, I felt it fiercely. It felt, to me, that Melody had taken Kane from me.

And it felt very wrong.

There was a sharp, bright knock.

I eyed my door warily, but I had no choice but to push off my covers, shove my feet into slippers, wrap my robe around me and shuffle toward the door.

Gwen stood there, decked out in new, low-riding jeans and a pretty blue blouse that plunged dangerously low at her neckline (too low to be around vampires, I thought wryly, but I knew that my best friend had no idea what this house was currently inhabited by). Her little traveling purse was on her shoulder, and her feet were currently being tortured by bright blue high heels that not even a stunt walker would probably try.

"Rose, you're not even *dressed*!" she sighed in exasperation, casting her eyes heavenward in a what-am-I-supposed-to-do-with-you expression of longsuffering. She pushed past me into my bedroom and began pulling out drawers on the antique wardrobe. "There's a *ton* of stuff I want to show you in Eternal Cove, and we don't have all day!" she muttered, pulling out jeans and panties. "Well, actually, we *do* have all day," she announced brightly, throwing a shirt in my direction. I caught it without thinking. "But there's a *lot* of stuff to see. Chop, chop! Put this on! Five seconds or less, missy!"

Oh yes. Right. Gwen and I had decided last night that we were going to go to Eternal Cove together so that she could actually show me around the little town I was now calling home.

But that was before…everything.

"Gwen, I don't actually think…" I began, but Gwen turned to me, putting her hands on her hips and raising an eyebrow. Her crazy brunette hair was teased even more than usual, and stood out from around her head as if she'd stuck her finger into an electric outlet. It was not without its charms.

"You are *not* backing out on me, missy—I don't care if you're hung over or whatever," she said with no sympathy, placing her hands at the small of my back, shoving the jeans and other things she'd chosen for me into my arms and then shoving me through my small bathroom door. She shut it behind me with a *thud* of finality. "And don't come out until you're ready!" she announced from the other side.

As much as I love my best friend—and trust me, she's saved my life a couple of times, and I love her a *lot*—I couldn't fathom gathering enough energy for a fun girl's night—or day—out. After all, let's be honest: Gwen wanted to show me a town I wasn't even certain I should be living in anymore.

As I stared at myself in the small bathroom mirror after flicking on the light, I saw my reflection's eyes narrow. Mirrors. That was odd. I sort of remembered something strange that had happened with mirrors, something like a dream, maybe *from* a dream…

"I don't hear you moving around in there!" was Gwen's utterly ridiculous comment from the other side of the door. "How hung over *are* you?"

Gwen had rearranged heaven and earth to help me move to Eternal Cove, *including* getting me the job at the Sullivan Hotel sight unseen—I hadn't even had to *interview*, Kane had trusted her so completely. Yes, I was miserable, but it was the right thing to do to keep my promise to her.

I sighed, washed my face and brushed my teeth, and threw on my clothes, pulling my hair into a ponytail. My long, red hair, usually fine and tangled *anyway*, was especially tangled after such a restless night, so I yanked a brush through the finalized ponytail and adjusted it in the mirror. I didn't have the heart to put on any makeup, but at least I didn't look—after I'd scrubbed my face—like I'd cried all night. Which I most certainly had. So I guess that was a start.

I opened the door and Gwen wrapped an arm in mine, practically dragging me to the door. I snatched up my skeleton key from the table beside the door and grabbed my coat, and then we were out in the hall and practically to the stairs before I could blink.

"I'll drive!" she sang out.

As we began to descend the spiral staircase, my heart seized. I didn't want to run into Kane. Frankly, I didn't want any *possibility* of running into Kane, and if I saw Melody first thing that morning, with her smug smile and dark eyes and hands all over Kane, I figured I'd probably die on the spot. Though Kane had certainly not paid any attention to me last night after Melody had showed up, I didn't want to talk to her about the events of the evening just yet. And I would do *anything* not to see the smirking, self-assured Melody ever again.

"Is there a way out to the parking lot from the basement?" I murmured quietly to Gwen.

This was the first moment that she cast a sidelong glance at me oddly—I think she was finally realizing that something wasn't right.

"Yeah, there's a couple of doors out from the

kitchen," she said, wrinkling her nose as she stared at me with wide eyes. "Rose, what's going on?"

"Oh, you know," I muttered, glancing ahead and down the staircase to see if anyone else was on it. Thankfully, there was no one. "The usual," I sighed.

"Huh," is what Gwen snorted, but made no other reply. When we hit the ground floor, we kept going all the way down to the basement.

The kitchens—empty the night before—were now bustling with the impressive energy of one lone woman. She stood a little shorter than me, her petite body curvy and very pretty beneath her knee-length pink dress with a scooped collar, showing off her pearl necklace. Her blonde hair was in two ponytails that dangled around her face as she stuck a finger in a metal bowl on the table and licked it with a thoughtful expression on her face. She wore a little makeup, and her full, bright pink lips seemed like they turned up at the corners pretty often.

"Molly, this is Rose," said Gwen, as we passed through the kitchens, toward the far half-glass door that seemed to be radiating sunshine from down concrete steps. "Rose, this is Molly—she's our cook and does a ton of other stuff at the hotel."

Molly snorted at that, licking her finger completely clean before offering me her hand to shake. I grinned a little and took it—her smile was infectious.

"It's so nice to meet you, Rose! I've heard so much about you, all good things, I promise," she winked. "So how are you enjoying yourself here so far? It's an easy job, isn't it?" she continued, steamrolling over anything I might have said. "They're so easy going, those Sullivan women, and they're just the nicest, the whole lot of them. I know you haven't been here long, but I want you to hear from me first, so I've got to tell you: I'm pretty sure they're *all gay*, and that's pretty great, I think, and I'm trying to get at least one, maybe two to give me a go, because I only took this job here because a friend of mine told me a rumor that they were all lesbian, and who wouldn't want to work at an all-lesbian place if you're a lesbian? I mean, it's—"

"Molly, we're kind of late—but we'll come back for dinner, yeah?" asked Gwen, all but shoving me at the small of my back again as she continued to push me through the kitchens and toward the door.

"If you're going to the Cove, for the love of whiskey, get me a latte!" Molly called over her shoulder as she took another finger-full of whatever she'd been whipping up (I was pretty certain it was cake batter), and licked it again with a thoughtful expression on her pretty face.

"I love her," Gwen murmured as she shut the door behind us and began trotting up the concrete steps toward the parking lot, "but she will literally talk your ear off if you let her. *Literally*. I don't even know if I *have* ears anymore, can you check for me?" She turned her head to me with a laugh.

I chuckled a little at that and drew my light jacket tighter about myself. It was a beautiful October day, the kind that people say you only get in Vermont, but I know that's not true. We had plenty of beautiful fall days in New Hampshire, too, and Maine was proving to be pretty similar in all the rich, gorgeous fall colors, crisp breezes and brilliant blue skies that contrasted so well with the breathtaking crimson of all the maples. The maple trees around the edge of the Sullivan Hotel were that bright red, now, and as we moved through the gravel parking lot toward Moochie,

Gwen's beat-up blue van that had somehow survived several years as her only transportation, a brisk wind began to move through the trees, making them shake their leafy heads and bringing with the wind the distinct nippy chill of a brisk fall day.

As Gwen unlocked her driver's side door, I drew the jacket even closer about myself, stood on tiptoes and peered over the far hedge wall that I knew separated most of the parking lot from the cliff path and the ocean.

The rolling blue far out to sea had high, white breakers that seemed to roll endlessly, and the prick of salt tickled my nose. It was beautiful—breathtaking, even, that view.

But it held no joy for me today like it should have.

"Okay," said Gwen, one brow up imperiously once I was in the passenger's side seat, clicking my seatbelt on. "You've got to spill."

"Spill what?" I asked. My voice sounded falsely bright, even to me. Gwen rolled her eyes so hard, her head seemed to roll with them.

"What. The hell. Happened?" she asked, dropping her van keys with a metallic jangle onto her jean-covered lap and folding her arms with an expectant sigh.

I gazed out at the ocean again, working my jaw.

Well. I didn't really have to mention anything about *vampires*.

"Remember…" I cleared my throat when it came out like a croak. "Remember how I told you last night that I was attracted to Kane?"

"Yes," said Gwen, drawing out the word as her other brow rose to accompany the first one.

"Whoa...did you..." She trailed off, blinking. "Did you get together with her?" she whispered.

"Yes. No. No..." I muttered miserably, placing my face in my hands and massaging my forehead with my fingertips. "There was a...complication." I licked my lips and thought, ruefully, *like the fact that she's a vampire, and I'm a human, and if you've ever seen any sort of television show or read a book about a vampire and a human together, when has that ever really worked out for the best?* "Her...her ex came back last night." I wracked my brains as I tried to figure out the easiest way to translate the fact that Kane's *long dead* ex-*soul mate* had seemingly *come back from the dead* to make out with her on a beach last night, just moments after I'd had that remarkable pleasure. I moved my hands down to massage the back of my neck, making sure my scarf was still hiding the small wounds. I grimaced as I glanced sidelong at my best friend. My best friend who was staring at me with her mouth open.

"Are you serious?" asked Gwen quietly. "I thought her ex was...well. Dead."

Why was I always the last to know about *everything*? I sighed in exasperation and shook my head, leaning back against the plush softness of Moochie's seat. "Yeah, well," I muttered, "I guess she wasn't as dead as everyone thought she was."

"Honey, you know I love you, right?" asked Gwen after whistling lowly. "But you attract trouble like honey and picnic baskets attract bears. What the *hell*? Her ex, who—by the way if I remember correctly—she pined over for *years* comes back from the dead when—"

"When I was kissing her on the beach," I groaned, putting my head in my hands again, and pressing my palms to my eye sockets so hard I began to see purple. "God, it was *terrible*," I groaned again, but then tears began to force their way between my sore eyelids, and I was holding back a sob.

"Honey, honey..." said Gwen, leaning over, and then she was squeezing me tightly, her warm arms wrapped around me with the same fierce strength she'd had when Anna died. "I mean, it was just bad luck, right? It's okay...I know you really had a thing for Kane, but you just got here, yeah? Lots of other fish in the sea. Er. Hotel."

I sighed for a long moment. Gwen was understanding and wonderful and the most caring best friend that anyone could have ever asked for. And I know she'd been wanting me to move on with my life—and my love life—after an acceptable mourning period following my girlfriend's accident and death. But I wasn't like...that. I wasn't the type to jump from woman to woman—I'd *never* been that type. There had been something in Kane that spoke to me, and Kane had said the same on the beach last night, that there'd been something in *me* that spoke to *her*. I drew in a shaky breath as I remembered: *From the very first moment I met you, touched you, there has been something in me that is answered by you...*

Though I had learned that the women (the *vampire* women, I reminded myself with a small sigh) in the Sullivan Hotel were lesbians, it didn't mean that I could move from Kane to someone else, quick as you please.

My brain and heart were subdued, for a small moment, by an image of Tommie that flashed before my eyes. Tommie with her smug grin and confidant eyes and how she'd straddled that woman last night, licking her lips as she licked her neck...

I sat back in the passenger side seat as Gwen straightened, too, searching my eyes. Tommie was gorgeous, and she was sexy, but she wasn't Kane. Yes, my body responded to Kane—I think *anyone's* body would have responded to Kane. But my heart called to her, and somehow, impossibly, a deeper part of myself called to her, too.

And now that would never be.

"I'm sorry I'm a little maudlin today," I told Gwen by way of apology. "I'm going to try to have a good time, but I...have a lot on my mind."

Gwen's mouth twisted into a frown. "I'm going to force you to have a good time," she promised, picking up her key ring and starting Moochie's engine. It grumbled to life, the van shuddering beneath us. "I want you to count your blessings," said Gwen, then, as she began to roll the van out of the parking lot.

I snorted in spite of myself. I...really couldn't think of anything to be grateful for. I hadn't exactly had an incredible or amazing life before moving to Eternal Cove, but at least it had been my own. Now I was living in a hotel full of vampires, the vampire I was drawn to desperately had just had her dead ex-lover appear out of the blue...

What, *really*, did I have to be grateful for?

"It's a beautiful day?" I tried, thought it came out a little grumbly as I stared out the window with a sigh. "Gwen, do I really have to—"

"What else?" asked my relentless best friend sternly.

"I'm grateful for you," I muttered, but this came out with a little bit less of a grumble. Gwen shot me a sidelong smile and nodded, prompting me to continue.

"I really can't think of anything else," I told her, watching the brilliant trees roll past. It really *was* a beautiful day, but I was in no mood to enjoy anything.

"Can I tell you something?" asked Gwen in that little conspirator's voice she'd had back in college when she'd try to set me up with the sexy female bartenders at one of the local dives. I sighed. I knew that tone.

"Yes?"

"When you came to me last night and told me that you were attracted to Kane..." She trailed off and put on her turn signal as she crawled to a stop before Eternal Cove's first light. The trip down the hill had been shorter than I'd remembered it. "I really thought you were going to tell me you were attracted to Tommie...not Kane."

I snorted with laughter before I realized she was being serious. I was speechless, then flustered as I tried to come up with a verbal reason of why absolutely, positively Tommie wasn't right for me.

As if she'd want me anyway. I remembered the blonde last night, practically writhing beneath Tommie.

I probably wasn't her type.

"I want a relationship," I pointed out to Gwen, then. "I don't want a one-night stand."

"Why do you think Tommie's not capable of a relationship?" Gwen snorted. The town of Eternal Cove spread out before us with its colorful, quaint shops and myriad of open parking spaces, even on a Saturday. She eased into an empty parking spot along the main street.

"Because I don't think she is," I said adamantly, shaking my head as I swung my purse up on my shoulder and hopped out of the passenger side, shutting the door firmly behind me.

"Rose, you're kind of old fashioned," said Gwen, then, trotting forward and putting an arm around my shoulder, gesturing with her other hand at the town. "And you've come to a sort of old fashioned place, which is great. But you want this sort of old fashioned love, with a woman coming along and sweeping you off your feet, the kind of love they put in storybooks. I'm not saying it can't happen," she interjected, holding up a finger when I began to protest, "but I don't know if you'll be satisfied with *any* woman." Her voice dropped to a whisper as she searched my eyes. "You told me, once, that you weren't even satisfied with Anna."

I remembered that conversation, even as the blush rose on my cheeks. Anna had been away for the weekend to visit her favorite aunt in the Bay, and Gwen had come over for a "weekend-long girl party," which was really only an excuse to drink a lot and try to make home-made ice cream from a recipe she'd found on the internet. I'd had one too many mixed drinks, and then I was pouring out my problems to Gwen, because she'd always been the one I could tell anything to. And yes—I'd told her that I loved Anna, and I wanted to spend the rest of my life with Anna…but sometimes, in the dead of night, I'd wake up from a dream I couldn't quite remember, glance over at my girlfriend who lay, sleeping and beautiful and breathing evenly, and think that being with her wasn't quite right.

Gwen was searching my face as she stepped forward, as she placed her fingers on my shoulders and shook me a little with a small frown. "Rose, you can't spend the rest of your life waiting for something perfect. 'Perfect' will never actually happen. Find a woman who makes you happy and settle down with her. Life's short. Don't spend it waiting for a storybook romance. There's no such thing."

I didn't agree. I knew that, as I stared into her eyes, too, unflinchingly. She was right, of course. I *did* want perfect. I wanted the type of love that would make every morning, no matter what the weather was doing outside, beautiful. I wanted the type of love that grew with time, that never waned. I wanted the type of love that made my heart rush ten years from now, twenty years from now. I wanted the type of love that made my body turn when she entered the room, that made every cell in my being drawn to hers.

I'd always wanted that. And I wouldn't stop wanting it.

And, if I was being perfectly truthful, there had been something in Kane...something that seemed like that sort of love was starting.

But I shook my head as Gwen stepped back, as we began to walk along the old, uneven sidewalk.

"Tommie told me you were cute this morning. She was in the kitchen, and we ran into each other," said Gwen quickly when I glanced at her with wide eyes. "She wanted to know if you were taken. And I took the liberty to tell her you weren't."

I worked my jaw, biting at my lip hard enough to keep my mouth shut. I loved Gwen, heaven knows I love her, but she'd always been a meddler in my love life. "But I'd just told you last night I was attracted to Kane—"

"Well, yes," said Gwen, smiling innocently. "But it's not like you're in a relationship with her. And, if Melody really *has* come back..." She trailed off, gazed into a shop window. "Then you're not *going* to be in a relationship with her."

It was painful and honest, that truth. I gazed into the shop window, too. It was a vintage clothing shop, and the old mannequin in the window display was sporting a beautiful aqua-colored dress with a wide yellow belt, a pair of yellow pumps discarded at the base of the mannequin, as if the woman wearing them had tossed them off and run off barefoot. My brain noticed those details, but my heart didn't.

My heart was thinking about Kane. About her full, cold lips, her brilliant blue eyes. The tilt of her head as she stared at me across the room, her gaze so intense that it burned with cold fire, taking a pull from her cigarette, clasped in long, elegant fingers...

"It just doesn't seem right, somehow," I told Gwen softly, fingering my purse's strap without thinking. "I don't understand why Melody came back. Tommie told me yesterday that she was *dead*. I mean, that's not something you really come back from. So what happened? Why is she back? And why did she come back at the exact wrong moment?" I swallowed back the tears that immediately threatened to erupt from my eyes. I took a deep, quivering breath, as Gwen and I began to walk down the sidewalk again. "It just doesn't make any sense. There was something about Kane..." I murmured.

Gwen walked beside me silently for a moment. She didn't have a good explanation for the coming-back-from-the-dead thing any better than I did. So she steered the conversation away from it. "Well, we're using today to forget about your troubles," said Gwen, affectionately draping an arm around my shoulder again. "Welcome to Eternal Cove, honey!"

It really was a beautiful, quaint little town.

There were old shops and buildings lining the main street that was filled with the scent of salt. The buildings were painted in bright colors, and though things were pretty shabby, they also seemed remarkably charming. The little book store we passed, a hand-written sign in the window proudly declaring that science-fiction was half off today, had the book store's name, *Eternal Tales,* hand-painted on a piece of driftwood that swung in the wind over the main door to the shop. The sign was hand-painted, like I remembered the sign welcoming us to Eternal Cove had been. It was little details like that that made me like the little town almost immediately.

Technically, I shouldn't have liked it, I shouldn't have relaxed my guard enough to like it, because I should have been deciding if I wanted to stay here or not. But I knew I shouldn't bring up that consideration to Gwen. She'd done so much to get me to move here, to restart my life, and I knew she'd be hurt and more than a little displeased that I was considering uprooting myself yet again to return to a place that had nothing for me either.

Maybe Eternal Cove had more surprises in store for me, I thought that day, gazing into the shop windows, eventually chuckling (though only a little) at my best friend's jokes as the lovely October sun swung lower in the sky.

But I really had no idea what surprises were yet to come.

❦

"Are you *sure* you don't want to head back to town, go bar crawling?" asked Gwen as she shut down

Moochie's motor, palming the beat-up blue van's ring of keys and glancing sidelong at me in the dark. Her eyes were wide and imploring. "It'd only take a few minutes to go back down to town, and you could meet some of the people who live here—it'd be great, you could make new friends, have some *fun*," she offered.

I knew Gwen wanted, more than anything, to go out drinking, and though I'd been trying for the past couple of hours to get up the energy to visit some local dive bars and drink away all of my most recent sorrows (which would probably involve more alcohol than a body could take), it had been a very long day. I was even a little sunburned because the sun had been out in very full force for an October day, but that's the problem with redheads: we burn easily.

What I really wanted was my slippers, a cup of tea, a good book and a plush chair after a probably revoltingly long bubble bath where all my fingers and toes pruned.

I was turning into an old woman.

"I'm bushed," I told Gwen, shaking my head and offering an encouraging smile. "I had too much fun today!" I teased her with a grin. "But that doesn't mean you can't go have *even more* fun, I mean, isn't that what Saturdays are for? Why don't you leave Moochie here, walk back to town—it's less than a mile or so, isn't it? You can go to the bars—weren't you saying at that one bar, you were friends with the bartender?"

"Free shots," Gwen sighed wistfully, staring in her rearview mirror at the lights of the town rolling away below the parking lot of the Sullivan Hotel through the trees.

"You should totally go," I told her resolutely, unlocking my seatbelt, and fishing around behind me for my one lone shopping bag, a paper bag containing a scarf I'd found at Eternal Cove's little second hand shop. Winter was on its way, and the bright purple scarf would go well with my red winter coat. "You'll have fun," I told her firmly, "and I don't want to be a wet blanket. I want you to go have fun—we had a really awesome day, and you deserve the cherry on top."

Gwen pocketed her keys and nodded, opening up the driver's side door. "You know, I think I'm going to do it," she said, shoving her hands into her pockets, too, with a grin. We both got out of the van, and Gwen locked the doors, pulling her jacket snugly around her shoulders. "Are you sure you don't want me to head back with you?" she asked, wavering, jerking her thumb up at the impressive red stone structure. The Sullivan Hotel seemed to be glaring down at us in the half-full parking lot. More guests seemed to have checked in while we were gone that day. "We could get food from the kitchens, paint our toenails..." Gwen trailed off. She didn't sound excited about these prospects *at all*.

"Go back to town," I urged her, crossing my arms against the chill wind that blew off the ocean. "I'll see you tomorrow."

"Okay," she said with a big smile, already walking away across the parking lot and toward the road. "It was a great day! We should do it again!" she called over her shoulder.

"Have fun!" I yelled back, and then I turned, staring up at the Sullivan Hotel.

I hadn't exactly forgotten my troubles that day, but the innocence of shopping, of laughing in the coffee shop...it had made me misplace my worries, if only for a little while.

It had been…nice.

But now here they were again, all wrapped up in the nice, neat little package that was the Sullivan Hotel.

I sighed, hitching my purse strap up higher on my shoulder, and began to make my way toward the entrance to the hotel, with its shadowy columns and gargoyle-bedecked red marble planters that were sized just big enough to contain dead bodies. That had been my very first thought upon entering the Sullivan Hotel, and it wasn't exactly forgotten now that I knew the hotel was full of *vampires*. I skirted the sprawling planters and ascended the few steps. The front lamp over the door was on, a few large moths bumping lazily on the glass, and a bright glow filled the porch as I made my way toward it.

A soft, sweet salt breeze angled its way in front of my nose, spiraling up from the ocean, and, for a moment, I had half a mind to make my way down the cliff path and take a night stroll on the beach. It would be very cold, but probably worth it—the moon was out, and it wasn't full yet, but its gibbous bulk swung low in the sky, illuminating everything with a soft, heavenly light. It'd be so easy to put off facing my troubles for a few minutes more…

But I squared my shoulders, laid my hand on the antique doorknob, and opened the front door of the Sullivan Hotel.

There was no one in the front entryway, which was a sort of relief. I hadn't exactly expected Tommie with another woman, but I wouldn't have been surprised if I'd seen her. The entryway itself with its lush, comfortable couches, was empty, but there was a woman I didn't recognize behind the front desk. She had short, close-cropped brown hair, and she wore a soft, flowing cobalt blue dress that clung against her hips and draped gracefully around her knees. It was much too summery to be worn in such cold temperatures, but she looked perfectly comfortable as she glanced up at me over the edge of the novel she held in her well-manicured hands. She wore a little makeup, and her glasses, perched on the bridge of her nose, looked designer.

"Are you Rose?" she asked me with an easy smile, shutting the book and setting it on the counter as she hopped off the stool.

"I am, yes," I told her, returning the smile. I'd met a few vampires, and for some reason, this woman struck me as absolutely, positively human.

"I'm Clare, one of your new co-workers—it's really great to meet you," she gushed enthusiastically, and I thought she meant it. She pushed her glasses further up her nose and glanced down at a post-it note next to the guest book. "I was told to tell you that the minute you come in, Kane wants to see you—it's kind of urgent. She's been in her office all day, and she's probably still there," Clare said, gesturing down the hallway toward the stairs. "So…"

My heart leapt up into my throat, and I paused for a moment, my hands forming fists, my shopping bag handle practically cutting into my palm. "Where is her office?" I asked her, trying to keep my voice carefully neutral. I think I failed at this, however, because Clare's eyes widened, and she put her head to the side as she considered me.

"You go down the hallway, up the stairs, and she's on the second floor, first door on the right." Clare rattled off the directions as if she'd had to tell them to a few people recently. Then she leaned forward over the desk a little, her palms flat against the antique wood, as she frowned. "Rose, are you all right? You look a little pale."

"I'm fine," I lied automatically and straightened my shoulders. I had no idea what Kane wanted to say to me. That she wanted me to leave the hotel? That was the first thing that crossed my mind. That, after the awkwardness of kissing me and then having her lover come back from the grave, she didn't want any distractions around. But if that's what she wanted to tell me, maybe that was for the best.

Because being around Kane, around this impossible woman who drew me to her like a flame lures a moth...maybe this wasn't so good for me, too.

I breathed out, nodded to Clare and tried smiling at her, but it came out as a sort-of grimace. I slowly began to walk along the corridor of paintings, across the red and black tiles, toward the far staircase.

I climbed each step like I was heading to my death. I didn't want to leave the Sullivan Hotel. I did, but I didn't. Part of me knew that it would probably be for the best if I left this place, left it and all of its vampires and secrets and beautiful women behind. But the other half of me cried out at the very thought.

I knew I was torturing myself, circling the questions over and over again, but there were no easy answers.

I reached the second floor and walked woodenly, stiffly, to the first door on the right. Like the other doors on this floor, it was impressively carved with vines and tiny cherub faces peeking around carved violets in the well-polished dark wood, and as I stepped close to it, placing my knuckles over the wood of the door, I inhaled, my heart beating even faster.

I smelled the rich, earthy scent of cigarette smoke, and that beautiful aroma of jasmine and cool, intoxicating spice that seemed to cling to Kane's cool skin.

"Come in," came the velvet voice from the other side of the door.

I hadn't even knocked. Somehow, she simply knew I was there.

I opened the door.

Kane had stood, behind her desk, and she was staring at me now in the dusky confines of the room that was fogged with smoke. Smoke from countless cigarettes, the ends of which littered a cut-glass dish on the side of the ornate, mahogany desk. Behind her rose massive dark bookshelves, covered with thick, old tomes, the metal words stamped into their bindings almost glowing in the dark. A Tiffany lamp with a lampshade covered in cut, glass dragonflies that glittered with light, was the only source of illumination in the room.

And though the lamp was very beautiful, though the bookshelves were very impressive, and there were probably hundreds of antique books here, I hardly even saw any of it.

All I could do was stare at Kane.

I'd had thoughts, on the way up the stairs, that I could be around her without being irresistibly drawn to her. After all, I wasn't a prepubescent boy. I was a grown woman in her thirties, and I'd been around the block a couple of times. I knew self-control, and I happened to have quite a great deal of it. It was ridiculous to think that I couldn't be in the same room as Kane and not want her. But the room we were in now, her office, seemed smaller than I thought it'd be, and the space between us, even with the heavy antique desk between us, seemed to shrink, even though I didn't move, though Kane didn't move, though we stood, frozen as statues, gazing at one another.

She stared at me with those piercing blue eyes that seemed to flash, like lightning over the ocean before a storm, all crackling, intense energy that could destroy so much in an instant. My God, she was beautiful to me. The men's suit jacket lay along her curves and lines that I couldn't help but follow, her tapered, pale fingers gripped the edge of the desk, and her long, sweeping ponytail was drawn over her shoulder, brushing against the arm of her jacket, the white-blonde hair looking so soft, so inviting, I wanted to step forward and touch it, stroke my fingers through it, press my lips to its satin.

But then she was striding out from around the edge of the desk, and the door was shut behind me, and my purse and my shopping bag fell to the floor as Kane's cold, long fingers curled around my upper arms, and her fierce gaze pinned me to the spot.

She searched my eyes as I stared up at her, as my heartbeat, burning too fast through my body, made me shudder beneath that gaze.

I couldn't speak. I knew that if I did, if my mouth tasted her name, it would all be over. And I wouldn't do that to her.

I already loved her too much to cause her any pain.

Instead, Kane was the one who spoke. She let go of my arms, even as my heart cried out for the loss of that brief contact. She took a step back, and then she was leaning against the desk, raking those long fingers through her white-blonde hair as she gazed at me with that same fierce expression.

"I'm sorry," was what she told me, then.

And her voice was so low, so sad, it tore me apart.

"Kane," I said, because I had to. My lips spoke her name, and my heart sank in me as I held out my hands to her, palms up. "What we...what we had. What we were beginning..." The words sounded strange to me. I didn't know exactly how to phrase it. What we'd started? What that kiss, last night, had started? I cleared my throat, breathed out for a long moment, closed my eyes, because I couldn't look at her anymore, couldn't look at those intense blue eyes that seemed to pin me in place, couldn't look at the curves of her hips, half-hidden beneath her suit jacket, but that I'd felt last night, my fingers curling around them as if it was the most natural thing in the world for my hands to be against her skin.

"Is it over?" I whispered.

I opened my eyes after a long moment in which there was only silence. My cheeks had begun to burn. Had I been projecting? Had the kiss been nothing more than a kiss? But no, she'd said things last night, and it didn't matter if Melody had come, she'd *still* said them. I would have their memory forever, no matter what.

And despite Melody's appearance, last night something had begun, and I had a right to know if it was over now.

She stared at me as she worked her jaw, the muscles clenching beneath that too-pale skin. Those devastating eyes were wet, and she glanced away from me, blinking back tears as her pink tongue darted out and wet her lips. Kane leaned back on her hands against the desk, her shoulders curling toward me, even as my own eyes were drawn to her chest, to the creamy shirt beneath the suit jacket, the tie that seemed to curve toward me, over her breasts. I swallowed, breathed out, fisted my hands and let them fall to my sides.

My entire body angled toward her as if she was the sun and I was the Earth, caught effortlessly in her gravity.

"Rose," she whispered, and I stared at her, felt my own eyes filling with tears, but I blinked them back furiously.

I stood, and I waited.

"Rose, it's..." She trailed off, glanced sideways, her jaw working again as she cleared her throat. "Melody and I...we have a history," she said then, pushing off from the desk, taking a single step toward me with a hand out to me. She paused when I didn't take it, when I stood still and listened. She dropped her hand, the fingers brushing against her pant leg as she sighed. "I thought Melody was dead," said Kane softly. "She was supposed to be. But she is no longer, it seems. She is, in fact, a vampire," she said, and there was a slight chuckle to the end of the words, but there was no humor in it. She continued to search my face, my eyes, as she spoke those words.

Melody had become a vampire?

If she hadn't died when she was supposed to, then where had she been all these years when Kane was in mourning?

Something felt not quite right.

Kane shook her head, took another step toward me. Her cool body was now close enough to touch if I could gather the courage to sweep up my hand, tuck a loose strand of impossibly soft white-blonde hair behind the luminous shell of her ear. But I stayed still. I listened, even as I bit my lip hard enough to draw blood. I tasted metal in my mouth, and Kane stared at me with those perfect blue eyes.

Stared at me, and pinned me into place.

"I wasn't toying with you," she said then, and it sounded so tired, even to my ears. "I want you to know that. What I said to you last night…it was all true. All true," she repeats. "I am drawn to you." Her voice had dropped even lower, was husky and smoky and smooth, and my entire body shuddered beneath that sound, even as she took a step closer, close enough now that when my breath came out, shaky and small between us, I could see it uncurling and unfurling in front of us like a ghost. Kane was so cold that I could feel the chill of her, even a few inches away. I could breathe in the scent of her, the scent of the cigarettes, the spice of her.

"I know you weren't toying with me," I said softly, the words coming out broken. I closed my eyes. It hurt too much to look at her, at her handsome, hard beauty.

Then, my hand in a fist at my side felt too cold. Her fingers were curled around my wrist, and they burned there, against my skin, but then she was raising my hand toward her mouth, and I was gazing up into those too-blue eyes again as she brought those perfect cold lips against the skin of the back of my hand.

And she kissed me there, as she gazed down and into my eyes with a gaze so fierce and full of longing, I found that I could no longer breathe.

"I must tell you," she said then, her smoky

voice so quiet, I strained to hear her, even as those full, lovely lips moved to the words. "Every night," she said, and a low, broken sob seemed to be caught in her throat as she blinked back tears again. "Every night," she tried again, licking her lips as I watched her, mesmerized, "I have dreamed of this impossible thing. Of Melody finally returning to me after all those years. Of how it would be when I picked her up, lifted her and held her to me as I turned around and around like a slow motion reunion scene from a movie," she choked back a laugh, but it was partially a sob. "It was a nightly dream," she whispered, searching my eyes. "Every night since she was taken from me, Rose, I dreamed of her returning," she said.

I waited, my heart beating so fast that its thunder and her voice were all I could hear, the gravity of her deep blue eyes the only thing I could see.

The pain and hope unfurling in my heart the only thing I could feel.

"But last night, for the first time in a very long time, I did not have that dream," she murmured. I realized, at that moment, how close her face was to mine, how close those cold, full lips were to my own. I closed my eyes and inhaled the scent of her, inhaled the coolness of her mixing with my own heat.

"Last night," she whispered, her chill lips against my cheek, my body trembling beneath that feather-light touch. "Last night," she repeated, voice low and husky and strong, "I dreamed of *you*."

My breathing came too quickly, my heart beating too fast. Her fingers were curled around my wrist and against my hand, and her cheek and lips were pressed to the side of my face as she breathed.

I wanted to stay in that moment forever. That

one, singular, *perfect* moment where nothing in the outside world with all of its troubles and problems could reach us, where we stayed in the small, dark sanctuary of her office and we were the only two people in the entire universe.

But moments come and go, and perfect moments leave us even faster.

The door behind me opened, the hinge creaking as the heavy wood was pushed inward slowly.

Kane straightened, gazing over my shoulder as her brows, furrowed from her confession, smoothed, and as I gazed up into her bright eyes, I saw her gaze shift, saw her expression change.

Pain passed over her face unmistakably.

"Melody," she whispered, and the pain was replaced, smoothly and easily, with an expression I could not quite read as I turned, taking in this beautiful creature who stood behind me, glaring daggers into my back. I'd wanted so much, after last night, to never see her again, but it was a childish want. If we were both going to be living in the Sullivan Hotel, we were probably going to be seeing more of each other than we would ever want.

In the light of the lovely Tiffany lamp, Melody was more beautiful than I remembered her on the beach last night. Of course, last night, I'd had only the light of the stars to see her by. Here, now, in the lamplight, I could clearly see her soft, creamy skin, her long, wavy red hair, wavier and redder than my own, and her sumptuous scarlet mouth. Now, her curvy body was encased not in a flimsy, gauzy nightgown, but in a bright red dress that was knee-length, but low in the front, showing off her womanly assets with curvaceous abundance. Her soft arms were crossed in front of her, and her long red nails were painted the same red as the dress, and glittered dangerously in the light. It was so strange, looking at her face, at her gracefully curving nose, her wide mouth with its full lips and her flashing green eyes.

It was like seeing a ghost.

She was beautiful, but there was something so strange about her. I couldn't place my finger on what about her made me uncomfortable...I just was.

Maybe it was how oddly familiar she was...

"Melody," said Kane's smoky, smooth voice. The woman, whose bright green eyes were pinned to me, straightened a little, her brows raising as she walked past me into the room, her hips swaying. She walked past me as if I wasn't even there, her hip brushing against mine not in sensual contact, but rather a bump. A bump that was crystal clear: *leave*.

"I missed you, baby," Melody whispered, her voice feather-soft as she reached up her lovely arms to wrap them around Kane's neck, drawing the tall vampire down into an immediate kiss.

And it was a very...heavy kiss.

I backed up. I could think of nothing else to say to Kane, and it was quite obvious that our talk was over. My eyes blurred by tears, I backed out of the room and pulled the heavy door shut behind me with a *click*. The last image I had of the two of them was Melody wrapped around Kane, of Kane's eyes closed and Kane's cold, long-fingered hands gripping Melody's hips. And of Melody's eyes open and narrowed in a grim smugness as she stared right at me, drinking the vampire in.

It made me sick.

With a hand over my stomach and trying to

calm the fact that I wanted to sob, I began to walk briskly down the corridor. I needed some air.

Why had Kane wanted to speak with me? Hadn't it just made things worse?

She'd apparently dreamed of Melody every singe night since she'd gone. But, it bears repeating: if Melody was a vampire and had loved Kane so desperately, where the hell had she been all these years?

And if they *were* really soul mates, that sort of love doesn't just...stop. And it's certainly not put on pause for a couple of decades.

So why, after all these years, had Kane not dreamed of Melody last night?

Why had she dreamed of *me*?

There were too many questions and too much pain, and I was beginning to drive myself crazy with all of the uncertainty and hurt swirling in my heart.

I was walking so quickly and in such a haze of upset that I, of course, wasn't exactly paying attention to my surroundings. When I briskly rounded the corner in the hallway, I had no thought other than Kane.

Which is why I ran into Branna.

Literally.

"Oof!" said the vampire, still standing, even as I threatened to teeter backward. She grabbed my arms and held me steady, keeping me from reeling back, as she gazed down at me with concern.

From the very first moment I'd met Branna, or Bran as she'd told me with a smile to call her, I'd felt that she was one of the most wonderful women I'd ever meet in my entire life. Yes, she was a vampire, but that didn't seem to matter. There was something about her. She seemed so kind, and it's as if we'd known each other all our lives, how easily we fell to talking. Here and now, seeing her friendly face gaze down at me with concern, her brows drawn together and her kind eyes wide, it was more than I could take.

Slowly, softly, tears began to leak out of the corners of my eyes.

"What's the matter, Rose?" asked Bran, her mouth curving downward into a frown as her cold hands tightened around my arms. "Are you all right?"

"No," I told her. It was impossible to lie to Bran. "I'm not all right."

"Hm," she sighed, her head to the side, concern making her brow furrow. "Is it anything a good glass of brandy could cure?"

"I don't think so," I told her, shaking my head.

"Do you want to talk about it?"

I gazed into her large, brown eyes, my own wet with tears.

"Yes," I said simply.

"...I *want* to be happy for Kane," I finished, my hands curling around a large mug of tea, the steam curling off its surface bringing the fragrance of peppermint to my nose. "And I am," I added hastily. "But..."

Branna lounged easily in the red plush chair, her legs crossed at the knees, one long calf resting on her thigh like she was at a gentlemen's board meeting. She'd loosened her bowtie, and had set it on the mahogany table beside her chair, and her creamy shirt's top few buttons were undone. She was handsome and graceful, like Kane, but when I gazed at her, I felt nothing but admiration. It was strange, really. Bran was absolutely my type, but there wasn't a bit of attraction there.

She'd just listened as I'd poured out my heart to her, making tea over the fire in an old-fashioned kettle and pouring the water into a generous blue pottery mug and over the peppermint leaves that had lain, curled in the bottom. We'd gone to her apartments to talk, and we'd remained in her living quarters, a beautiful room with tall ceilings, and very old wallpaper covered in faded blossoms. Everything in the room was antique and well cared for, and I'd felt immediately at home here.

Branna sighed and uncrossed and recrossed her long legs, working her knuckles under her jaw as she thought for a long moment. "I must admit," she said quietly, "Melody is quite different from how I remember her. Kane brought her to our study this morning, and it..." She trailed off, her brows furrowed as she grimaced. "It wasn't exactly like old times."

"I just want Kane to be happy," I said again, leaning forward, resting the mug's bottom in my lap as I adjusted my grip on the handle and, raising it, took a sip. "And Melody was supposed to be so important to her. Her...soul mate." The words went sour in my mouth.

Branna straightened at that, a wistful smile curling her lips. "Well, yes. Melody *was* Kane's soul mate. I've never seen two people more in love. They had this sort of...well. *Electricity* between them." Branna's head was to the side as she shook it. "That's why this isn't adding up. Melody has given us no explanation as to where she's been all these years other than 'detained.' The Melody I know would never have been 'detained' for so long and apart from Kane for so long. And she wouldn't be so...smug about returning." Branna frowned again. "I feel strange about it. I'm glad that you came to me. Kane didn't tell me about the fact that she didn't dream about Melody last night. She normally tells me everything..." She trailed off, her long fingers drifting around and around her own mug's rim.

"How long have you and Kane known each other?" I asked her, then.

Branna looked up, her lips curving into a smile. "Oh," she sighed, leaning back in her chair, her eyes gazing over the top of my head. "For a very long time," she told me. She glanced back down into my eyes again. "A *very* long time," she whispered. She gazed at my face, but she wasn't really seeing me. Her eyes were unfocused. It's as if she was staring into a window of memory...

She blinked, suddenly back in the room as she smiled. "Would you like me to tell you how Kane and I came to be..." She gestured down at herself and tapped her lips with a little chuckle, "the way we are?"

"Yes," I told her, the cool scent of peppermint unfurling in my mouth as I took another sip.

Bran leaned back in her chair, gazing up at the ceiling for a long moment.

"It began the day I died," she whispered.

A very long time ago, over three hundred years ago now if you'd believe it, we lived in Ireland. Kane and I grew up in a very small village near the coast where everyone knew everyone else, and it was such a hard life full of dawn to dusk work to survive, but we were content in it. Kane wasn't called Kane back then. Her mother had named her Mercy, the very last thing Kane's mother did before she passed, having brought her only child into the world.

Back then...well. It wasn't so easy to love women if you were a woman yourself. Mercy and I knew the truth of each other, and in the very beginning, when we were teenaged girls, we'd kissed one another in my father's thatched barn during a rainstorm, our very first kiss. We both agreed that this was what we wanted, but oh how we'd laughed after kissing each other. We both knew we wanted women, but we did not want each other. We became so close, after that. We were both comrades in a secret sort of society that contained only each other. And we kept those secrets close.

One day, I was out in the fields with Mercy. We were breaking up the sod, for it was March or so, and the winter had been treacherous and we needed to begin the planting, or there would be nothing to eat that year. I still remember those wants and worries. If you didn't plant your own food, you would be so hungry that winter, you might perish. My mother was a drunkard, and my father had gone on to meet his god when I was very small, so Mercy helped me with my fields often.

I remember that day. The sun was bright, but wan in the sky. There was the scent of spring in the air, of a quickening of green that I could almost taste, and energy surged through me as we methodically broke through the chunks of sod, making the dirt ready for the seeds.

Our village was out of the way of most of the major roads, so there was little more than a footpath that connected our village to the next one. But still, we heard the tell-tale creak of carriage wheels over tussocked meadow, and we both straightened, squinting into the sunlight.

There was a coach coming along that footpath. Two massive black horses pulled it, and the driver was cloaked and hooded in black, even in the fine daylight. The coach was black, black as Death's own coach, and as it trundled over the rutted earth, a chill passed over me.

We had stories, in old Ireland, of banshees—dark spirits--coming to scream at us when death approached, and it seemed, at that moment as we both straightened and looked at that black coach, that a faint scream came, shrill and sharp, into the air.

But there was no one around to have screamed it.

The massive coach with all of its fripperies and ornamentation creaked to a stop beside our stretch of field looking so wildly out of place that in any other situation, I might have laughed at it. The driver dismounted with a great leap from the top of the coach, which seemed almost impossible, as it was a good almost ten feet to the ground. It was almost otherworldly, the way that he leapt and then straightened, too, and he was opening up the door of the coach before we could even blink.

And out of that door was thrust a delicate, expensive black boot. And attached to that pretty little boot was a woman. She descended down onto the ground in a swirl of black cloth, for she was clothed in black from the top of her head, covered in a black veil, to those pointed black boots. She wore the sumptuous black gown of a gentlewoman or lady, and I knew by the big black horses and coach, coachmen and gown, that this was a very rich women. And rich women never *came to our part of the country.*

I felt a violent chill descend over my skin as she all but drifted over the broken sod, over the uneven ground that anyone would have had a difficult time walking over, as if she was as light as the angels themselves, her pretty, useless boots getting stuck in not a single rut. I'd been walking the fields my whole life, but I still tripped over them like a gangly calf.

She floated across the ground like the devil himself.

I could not see her eyes behind that heavy black veil.

But I knew from the angle of her body, the way she curved across the earth, that she was not looking at me.

She had eyes only for Mercy.

We didn't really have nobles, as you might call them now, in that area of Ireland back then. It was mostly very poor peasants, Irishmen trying to make their living by being a little more stubborn than the stubborn land itself. A lot of folk were heading over to America, even back then, and our own village had lost quite a few people to the lure of easier times in the golden land of opportunity. As such, we were only used to being around fellow peasants, weren't used to being around anyone of higher rank than us, which is why Mercy stood her ground as the woman drifted ever closer to her.

But there was something not quite right about the woman, and though I'd never been a superstitious person, I felt that there was more than a little something of the devil about this stranger. So I stepped closer to Mercy, tugged at her shirtsleeve.

"It's all right, Bran," she told me smoothly, her mouth in an insolent smile as she gazed at the stranger. "It's only a high and mighty lady come to see those who are beneath her."

The woman in her relentless approach of us paused.

And then, from beneath that black veil came laughter. High, piercing laughter that made my head ache, that sounded so sinister with its musicality and cruelty. It didn't sound human.

Mercy, beside me, stiffened, but didn't remove her gaze from the approaching woman. If possible, my friend's eyes flashed even brighter as she stared at this strange woman who floated across the rutted land toward us. Mercy's stance was wide, her hands at her sides curled into tight fists.

She was ready to fight if she had to. That was just Mercy's way. There had never been a single thing in the world that frightened her.

I wasn't exactly quaking in my boots, either. But there was fear in me as I stared at this stranger.

"Don't be afraid," the woman whispered, then, as if she could hear my very thoughts, and my knees grew weak at the sound of her words. My legs quaked, but I tried to be as strong as I could as the woman finally stopped, close enough for me to reach out and touch the lace of her garment. Mercy stood, leaning forward, her shoulders back, as she gazed at this woman with flashing eyes, defiance radiating from her.

"Who are you?" she demanded, and again, the woman laughed. I felt light-headed, as if I would fall against the sod, but I tried to stand firm.

But the sound of the woman didn't affect Mercy one bit.

She stood and did not waver.

"In all of my many years," the woman whispered, the sound sibilant and hissing like a snake as she stepped closer, as she wrapped her long, gloved fingers around Mercy's wrists, tugging her forward, *"I have never met a girl I could not seduce with a single thought. There is something in you. Something special. I would have you come to me and be mine."*

Mercy and I had often thought about the sort of girl we would want to have if we could even dream of such a thing. Mercy had told me, often, about a dream she had when she slept about a red-headed girl. There were a lot of red-headed girls where we lived, so we really thought nothing of it. But in all that Mercy had ever told me, she'd never spoken of this type of woman being something she was attracted to, someone dark and sinister and otherworldly.

And Mercy held true to this. For she did not budge. The woman tugged on her wrists, but Mercy stood where she was, feet planted firmly against the earth and shoulders back as her nostrils flared.

"I'm not going anywhere *with you,"* she said with finality.

"You love women. Do not deny it," the stranger hissed as she tugged on Mercy's wrists. *"And here in this miserable*

little cesspool of a village, this loving of women will get you killed. If you come with me, I will take you to a place where that's not even a consideration. Where you could be safe to be yourself. In my home, you can be anything you want to be." Her words were dripping with charm, and they made sense to me. I wanted to go with this woman, even though I hadn't even been asked. I would have followed her into the depths of hell if she'd asked, as my earlier thoughts about her, my bad feelings about her, seemed to have evaporated.

"No," Mercy persisted.

"Three times," whispered the woman, then, her voice darkening to a dangerous hiss. "Three times will I ask if you will come with me of your own free will. Three times will I ask, and only three, and if you do not say yes, I will simply take you."

Mercy leaned forward then, leaned forward with such crackling energy, I took a step back.

"You will never have me," was what she whispered.

It was then that the coachman stepped forward with his whip and his strong hands. He dealt a blow to the back of my head, and I do not know what they did with Mercy. But when I came to, we were in the coach with the strange woman.

And I no longer felt as if she was there to help us. Or that she was lovely. For the leather flaps had been rolled down over the coach windows, and in the darkness, she had removed her black lace veil.

She had long, unkempt black hair that did not shine in the subdued light but seemed to swallow any light that came near to her, and there was dried blood around her small, wrinkled mouth. And when she stared at me with her bright blue eyes that seemed to flash with raw power, I felt a shudder go through me.

Mercy though, beside me, was unafraid.

"Return us now," she growled.

The woman tilted back her head and laughed and laughed, a snarl at the end of every chuckle. "Why should I *return you?" she told us. "There is not a soul who will miss you, not a soul you have left behind that would not jump at the idea of having one less mouth to feed. Now you both belong to me." She leaned forward then, and she smiled.*

Her teeth that had been such perfectly normal, human teeth before, seemed to...grow, even as we watched, the old ivory color against her blood-red tongue lengthening, sharpening. And her incisors became as deadly and as sharp as a wolf's as she licked her lips and stared at us with evil, triumphant eyes.

We sat across from her in the coach, and she crossed that space between us in a heartbeat, as quick as death. In another heartbeat and without me even seeing the movement, she had her arms around Mercy's shoulders, hanging there, but it was not the passionate embrace of a lover. It was the sort of embrace an insolent cat does to a half-dead mouse right before it's about to devour it. She snapped back her head, and in the dull light of the coach, I saw her wet teeth flash as she opened her mouth wide and darted forward. She sunk her teeth into Mercy's neck, even as Mercy kicked and screamed, even as Mercy fought as furious as she-devil. I fought, too, but two girls against one monstrous woman was no match.

She bit us, and we bled, and she drank until there was nothing left to drink.

She drained us dry.

We were meant to die. She drained us on the way back to her castle like a light afternoon snack, and her evil coachman dumped our bodies down into the depths of her cellar when she returned, kicking out our corpses into a shaft that led down to the lowest cellar, which might be more appropriately dubbed her dungeon. So we fell there, but we were not alone, for our bodies collapsed beside the other, rotting corpses of the woman's gluttony, all young girls she'd lured with different stories, all young girls killed in the prime of her youth so that she could be satiated and satisfied and drunk from the blood of the innocent.

So we fell among the dead girls after we'd been drained dry, and we should have died.

So we did.

During the fight in the carriage, we had bit and scratched and kicked and punched, and a little bit of the woman's blood had spattered against our mouths and the ragged wounds in our necks that she'd inflicted with her teeth. Now, vampire blood is very strong. The cells seek a body like hunters themselves, for they crave to be inside a creature. We were drained dry, not a single drop of human blood remained within us.

But a few drops of vampire blood had gotten inside.

A few drops of vampire blood alone is not enough to save a human being or turn them from human into vampire. It needs to be a great amount of blood given freely from a vampire into a human in order to turn that human. But sometimes, when people are very, very strong or the will to live and fight again is raging through them, there is the slimmest of chances that a few drops of blood is enough to begin the change.

Some might call that a miracle, the odds are so against it.

But when Mercy and I woke a few days later, in the dark and the stench of that terrible, rotting cellar, we were...alive. We did not know what we were...we were hungry, I remember that. We were starving, and we were weak, but we were not really afraid. Not even when the pitiful bits of sunlight we could get fell down on us from a grate far above, and we saw that we were surrounded by the bones and bodies of countless dead girls. That these bodies, in fact, were all that the cellar contained.

That is when we knew who had taken us.

For years and years, the local villages had a bogeyman story that few adults believed, but what was always whispered to the children—especially the girls. For there were rumors that a gentlewoman named Darcy was stealing away girls from surrounding villages. There were rumors of what happened at her castle, rumors that she was using the blood of these innocents to bathe in, that she was eating their flesh as a cannibal. So mothers and fathers would tell their daughters to be good, or Darcy would get them. We'd heard the stories ourselves, growing up, but had never, ever believed they could be true.

But we knew the truth of it now.

Darcy was a vampire.

And she had drained us dry because she wished to kill us, to drink us up and satiate her desperate lust for blood.

And that meant, since we had died and come back to ourselves with this raging hunger in our bellies, we knew that we had become the damned, too.

Mercy and I were now vampires.

I wanted to leave that place. We knew what we were when we trembled and stumbled into the light, up and out of that cursed dungeon, alongside the crumbling stone walls of the castle, when the sunlight burned us as we stayed in it, burned us gently, but burned us nonetheless. When a deer crashed through the underbrush, and our incisors lengthened, we knew, truly, what we had become, then.

We followed and felled that deer and drained it dry, the two of us ripping into its warm muscles with sharp teeth, lapping at the blood like newborn kittens, unsure of how to drink. And then, full, I stood shaking and told Mercy: I wanted to leave. I asked Mercy for us both to go, for us both to run away, far away, where our families would never see what monstrous creatures we'd become, where we might be able to start again, hidden from the world who would never understand us.

But Mercy stood there, in the woods, blood dripping down her chin, her piercing blue eyes wide and wild.

"We cannot leave," she whispered, rubbing the back of her hand over her mouth and smearing the blood. She was shaking, but not with fear.

She was shaking with fury.

"We cannot leave until we stop her. She will not do this again to another girl," said Mercy, then. *"We will stop her."*

Oh, how Mercy was angry. Her life had been taken from her, her future, every possibility of happiness in the life we'd known and expected to have. We did not know at the time how much the world would change, and we did not know, at the time, what would become of us. We thought we had become damned. Cursed. That our very souls had been given to the devil in exchange for tormented immortal life. For all we knew were the stories of vampires, and we did not yet know the truth of the matter.

In all of this, we knew nothing.

But Mercy knew that we must stop Darcy.

So we went back into the dungeon, finding our way up through broken staircases and cracked doors as we rose ever higher into the castle itself, and we sought out the evil woman who had done this to us.

And we found her, about to kill another girl.

The vampire Darcy sat in one of the tall, crumbling towers that once must have been beautiful, back when this castle had been full of lords and ladies who ruled this area. Perhaps Darcy had even seen that time, for she sat before a long table in a massive dining hall as if she'd lived here her whole life, as if she was still the lady of this place. Her big black skirts billowed around her as she leaned back, gazing at the long table before her with narrowed eyes and a wickedly smiling mouth. She was the only one seated at that table, and tied to the table's surface as if she was the main course (and indeed, she was) lay a beautiful young girl, stripped of almost all of her garments save for the chemise that had been pushed down her shoulders.

This young thing had long, brunette hair and such a pretty face, but it was contorted in horror as she screamed and screamed. But these were not cries for help. They were the desperate strains of fear, because this poor thing knew how far Darcy's castle was away from any village or people, and she knew there was no one to hear her or save her.

No one but us.

Darcy had not been expecting us, and her coachman—her only servant—was down feeding the coach horses and bedding them down for the evening. So when we entered the room, bold as you please through the wide archway to the hall beyond and Darcy rose, standing slowly and turning her body to us, her bright blue eyes growing icy and wide and angry, she knew she was caught.

And that she was at an end.

Mercy was strong, and Mercy was angry as she strode forward so quickly, I almost didn't see her move. It was Mercy who killed Darcy. It was savage and ghoulish, but how else do you kill a vampire other than removing its head?

But when Mercy was done, blood covering the front of her, her hands dripping as she held the gory head before her, the girl who had been tied to the table began to scream again.

"No, no, it's all right—you're safe," said Mercy gently, and with a flick of her hands she'd cut through the ropes and untied them from the girl's body, but the girl leapt off the table and backed up against the far wall, shaking as she gazed at the two of us.

"You're monsters," the girl whispered. And then, over and over again like a mantra: "Please don't hurt me."

"We won't," Mercy promised her, but the girl was sobbing, was repeating the word "monsters" over and over again, then. She turned, and she fled past us out into the hallway.

Mercy dropped the vampire's head in disgust on the floor where it rolled to a standstill away from us. She knelt there, then, in the cool blood that pooled upon the stone floor, and with her face in her hands, Mercy began to weep.

I tried to console her. I tried to tell her that we were not the monstrous ones. That we had saved this girl's life, and the girl was upset, had just experienced a nightmare world that she could never understand. But there was something of truth in the girl's words, something that we both had to acknowledge.

We had become irrevocably changed. We were no longer human. We were vampire. And there was something in us that had made destroying Darcy so very easy.

There was something of Darcy in us, whether we wanted to admit it or not.

Mercy decided to change her name to Kane. Kane means "fighter," and she had fought so hard to live that it seemed appropriate. We took from the vampire's storehouse some money, some jewels, and we fled that land. We left Ireland, sailed on to England, and we changed our lives irrevocably, as they had been changed for us.

And we stayed together, Kane and I. And we vowed that though there was something monstrous in us, never again would it rise and consume us.

We would never become like Darcy.

Branna tilted her head as she gazed at me, as her eyes lost the soft focus of the past and saw me clearly again. "Though our past is steeped in blood, we have stayed true to that decision for our entire lives. Kane and I traveled the world together gathering women to us who were like us—and we all agreed, together, that we would never become like Darcy. At the same time, we knew that we would never again hide the most essential part of our natures: we would love women and there would be no shame in that, not like there was shame of being a vampire," said Bran with a sigh. "And, over time, we lost our shame of that, too. We know that we are not damned. We hurt no other creatures. We do not take what is not freely given," she murmured. "And eventually, Kane found Melody. And I am, perhaps," she said with a small smile, "still waiting for the woman who is right for me. And I think I shall find her. Someday." She bit her lip, cleared her throat. "But the love Kane and Melody had for each other...it is not what is reflected in what I see between Kane and Melody now. There is something rotten in the state of Denmark, my dear Rose," she whispered.

I thought about the story as I sank back in the plush chair, as I set my empty tea mug beside me on the little table. I thought of how strong Branna and Kane must have been to survive an ordeal like that.

But it didn't surprise me, this story of their strength.

Kane had always struck me as a fighter.

Branna still watched me with appraising eyes that narrowed after a quiet moment. "There was something between you, Rose. Between you and Kane," she whispered, then. "My question to you is...what are you going to do about it?"

I stood slowly, shook my head, smoothed out my skirts. "Thank you so much for the tea, Bran. And for the story. I loved hearing it," I told her sincerely. "But I'm not going to do anything about...about Kane and me. There's nothing there anymore." I worked my jaw and swallowed, but I had to say it. So I did. "Melody's back."

Branna stood, bowing her head to me. She looked as if she was going to say something else, but then she shook her head sharply, folded her hands in front of her. "If that's how you feel, Rose," she told me, her voice quiet.

It wasn't how I felt.

But there was nothing else I could do. I'd told myself that so many times that I was almost beginning to believe it.

But there was some small part in my heart that cried out against that.

If I was being honest with myself, I would have admitted that if Kane couldn't fight for me, then I wanted, more than anything, to fight for *her*.

"Did you hear?" whispered Clare when I came to stand beside her behind the front desk. It was the next day, morning, and I was well-dressed in a navy-blue blouse and black pencil skirt, ballet flats over tights, my hair up in a wavy ponytail. I didn't know exactly who I intended to impress anymore—the woman I was falling in love with, who I could no longer have, or the rest of the vampires.

I guess that was a little uncharitable. It seemed that most of them couldn't help that they were vampires.

But I'd gotten up on the wrong side of the bed that morning, so I was feeling a little less than charitable. Last night I'd been tortured with dream after dream of Kane, Kane in clothes I'd never seen her wear, antique clothes, her long white-blonde hair done up in antique hair styles, as if we were in another time. The dreams were full of Kane kissing me passionately, her cold mouth against mine as she drank me in. Kane had whispered in these dreams, over and over with her perfect, smoky voice that she loved me. So many different dreams and situations, but always the same thing. A long, sweet, hot kiss.

And then: "I love you."

I was driving myself crazy.

"Did I hear what?" I asked Clare, trying out a smile. It felt like a grimace, but it seemed to make Clare happy, for she returned the smile and looked a little relieved. She seemed like a nice woman, my new coworker. I liked her, even though I hadn't spent that much time with her. We were supposed to share a shift that day, so I thought I'd get to know her a little better.

It was Monday, and the Conference was supposed to begin that night. The Conference, I realized, that was the "big meeting" of vampires.

I doubted, though, that Clare's secret was telling me the Conference was full of vampires.

"Kane's ex-lover is back," she murmured out of the corner of her mouth with wide eyes. "And supposedly, she's starting to help Kane run the hotel again."

"Oh, joy," I muttered with a long sigh. I was a pretty easy-going person, and I'd once prided myself with the fact that I could get along with almost anyone.

I could not, however, imagine getting along with Melody.

Clare began to prattle on about hotel gossip, about the Sullivan women and normally this would interest me immensely—the mysterious Sullivan women were captivating to me with their interesting stories and, of course, the unexpected fact that they were all vampires. And it's not that I didn't want to listen to Clare or contribute to the conversation, but my mind was in other places, and my eyes had strayed to the painting on the wall by the front desk of Kane.

I knew it was Kane, now, the woman who

lounged with the big, black cat—possibly a panther or a jaguar. And though the cat was impressive and big and beautiful, you weren't looking at the cat when you glanced at the painting.

You were looking at the naked woman sitting regal and calm and utterly comfortable in her own power.

It was done tastefully, the woman's nudity, as classic art tended toward, with Kane in a classic pose, her back to the viewer, but as my eyes swept over the taut curves and lines of her body, even painted by a master's deft stroke, and knowing it was only paint, it was still bewitching to me.

I hadn't noticed that Clare had grown silent. I did notice, however, the elbow lightly jabbed into my stomach.

And then, as if summoned by my thoughts themselves, Kane was there, standing in front of the desk.

Clare elbowed me again, and I straightened, smiling wanly at the handsome vampire who leaned against the front desk lazily, her palms pressed against the wood and her upper body leaning toward me with a sort of languid ease, as if her entire body wasn't raw, incredible power. I'd not yet seen her power utilized, but it seemed as if I already knew what she was capable of.

I stared at her, at her bright blue eyes that seemed to be gazing into the deepest, darkest parts of me. We stayed that way for a long moment, long enough that Clare shifted her weight uncomfortably and cleared her throat.

"Clare, I'm sorry to interrupt you," said Kane smoothly, softly, an unlit cigarette suddenly in her long, tapered fingers. "But I need to borrow Rose just for a moment. Rose, if you don't mind." She straightened, and put the cigarette to her lips, drawing a silver lighter out of her pocket. It was a little absurd to see such a mundane contraption in her beautiful hands that all I could do was stare for a long moment. Then I straightened, too, and cleared my throat.

"I'll be right back," I told the open-mouthed Clare, and I walked woodenly around the edge of the front desk, falling beside Kane.

And we left through the front door, my heart racing. We walked together like we'd been doing it all our lives, Kane's hands in her jacket pockets, her shoulders rounded and her head bent, me keeping pace like my body knew what to do, even when my heart didn't.

The door shut behind us quietly, and then it was just Kane and me on the porch between the red columns and the red stone walls of the Sullivan Hotel itself. I realized I was disappointed with how beautiful the day was—I wanted it to be atmospheric, to be night with all its stars overhead, swinging bright and full of possibility in the sky again. But it was only morning, and the sun was out, almost hot and shining as already-fallen leaves skittered across the full gravel parking lot, and the sea breeze rose up from the chill ocean, making me taste salt.

Kane remained in the shadow of the marble column, leaning back against it as she inhaled deeply on her cigarette and let the breath out into the air like smoke, her nose pointed to the sky.

"I told Melody," she said, then, dropping her gaze and watching my face with her own inscrutable blue eyes as she flicked the ash off the end of the cigarette slowly. She took another long pull. The smoke curled out of her mouth as she murmured: "about us."

I went cold.

"There is no 'us,' Kane," I whispered almost immediately, my first reaction. It hurt to say it, and it twisted the knife in my gut to see Kane's gaze darken, to see her clench her jaw, but it was the truth, wasn't it?

There was no "us." Only Melody and Kane.

"What did you tell her?" I whispered, wrapping my arms around my middle. Though the day was warm, I felt a cool chill descend over me as Kane straightened, as she stepped forward toward me. My body betrayed me as it leaned toward her, but she moved past me, taking another long pull on the cigarette before stubbing it out against the side of the closest marble planter and depositing it in the cigarette post on the side of the door.

She stood so close, I could reach out and press my fingers against her cheek, press my palm there, and she might turn, might—if I was lucky—and she would press her lips against my skin.

Slowly, as if we were in one of my dreams again, she took a step forward, working her jaw, swallowing, wetting her lips as she searched for the words, her intense blue eyes pinning me into place. My body shuddered with surprise and delight even as her cold fingers curled over my hips, even as I closed my eyes, breathing out in pleasure. It was such a simple touch, but it was more than I'd ever expected again.

I should never have expected *anything*. But here we were. And the leaves danced across the parking lot as the low wind blew, and the scent of Kane swirled all around me, that bold note of jasmine, the intoxicating spice of her. I breathed her in as my heart ached, as every bit of me cried out for me to reach forward and touch her, too.

But then she spoke.

"I told her..." Kane's voice was low, gravelly, smoky as she struggled with the words, as the anguish spilled out of her mouth. I opened my eyes, gazed up at her as she breathed out, as she searched my face, tightening her grip on my hips as if I was the only thing that held her to this place, as if I was the only thing that anchored her to this world. "I told her that I am drawn to you. That there is something about you that calls to me so strongly I cannot ignore it." She gazed down at me with such deep longing that I almost moaned as her fingers dug into me. I wanted her, wanted her in ways I couldn't even understand. She whispered: "I told her that, after all this time, I don't understand what has happened...but what was within Melody that connected me to her. It's gone."

Kane searched my eyes and took a shaky breath, her own blue eyes wide and wet with tears. She pushed away from me, then, and I instantly ached as she straightened, shaking with self control as she tugged down on the hem of her jacket, transforming almost instantly from the vulnerable Kane who'd gripped me tightly, her voice and her body filled with desire, who told me with that perfect, smoky voice that she was drawn to me...to the Kane who ran the Sullivan Hotel, strong and electric and completely without weakness.

But the vulnerable pain remained in her, and I saw it clearly when she gazed into my eyes, searching to the very heart of me.

"This isn't going to work," she whispered, shaking her head as she turned away from me, her profile outlined by the brilliant sun as she turned toward the door. She brushed past me and for a brief moment, her fingers curled around mine and then were gone. "I can't be around you. Not without..." She choked on the words, straightened again, cleared her throat. "I'm not good for you. Please go," she murmured, her hand on the doorknob.

She paused for a long moment, her back stiff beneath my gaze, the lovely slope of her shoulders pain-filled and tight, and then Kane opened the door and was through it.

I hadn't even realized that tears leaked steadily out of my eyes. I reached up and brushed them angrily away.

Not good for me? Couldn't I be the judge of that? She'd made the decision to be with Melody—I'd been given no choice in this.

I followed her angrily. There were so many words that wanted to tumble out of my mouth, so many feelings raging through me, but mostly what I wanted was to stand up on my tiptoes, wrap my arms around her shoulders and kiss her so deeply that we'd merge, the two of us together.

But when I entered into the front lobby, Kane was, of course, already gone.

As I stood in the entryway, as my hands curled and uncurled into fists, anger moved through me. And of course I was angry. I had every right to be. Kane had told Melody about us? Why did she say, again, the words that pained me so much? That she was drawn to me. She'd made the choice to be with Melody. She had chosen Melody absolutely, and the pure and honest truth of the matter, the painful truth, was that she hadn't chosen me.

And we both had to live with that decision.

Clare watched me with wide eyes as I all but stomped around the edge of the front desk, pushing up the sleeves of my blouse as I cleared my throat, lifted up my chin, placed my hands flat on the surface of the front desk.

I stared at the front door and dared it to open with guests.

And, surprisingly, it did.

I hadn't even seen a car pull up when Kane and I were out there, but now on the front step, wheeling two taupe designer suitcases in behind them, were two women. One had hair the same color as Kane's, but it was much longer, descending to curl beneath her hips, and a cruel, insolent smile on her beautifully made-up face. She wore a stylish blouse and pencil skirt ensemble that seemed out of place with her long, unbound hair.

The other woman, like many of the people who had checked in, wore a plain black dress and a plain, black hat that reminded me of something women might have worn in the seventies on a beach. Her big, movie-star-dark sunglasses hid her eyes, but her face looked old, lined and wrinkled. Her thin slash of a mouth was still covered in red lipstick, however. She reminded me of an aging starlet, clinging to something she'd lost long ago, but when she angled her face toward me, I took an involuntary step backward. I couldn't see her eyes, but her face seemed, somehow...hungry.

"Magdalena and Cindy," said the white-blonde woman, her lips curling up at the corners as she watched my reaction. Startled, I gazed back at her. She was tapping the surface of the desk with an expensive-looking manicure.

Clare gave me a glance, but she began the necessary arrangements to find their reservations as I turned woodenly, stepping toward the back wall with its rows and rows of hooks and keys and fished two keys off the wall. The blonde woman signed "Magdalena" with a flourish of the pen and then handed the pen to her companion as she put her head to the side and smiled charmingly.

"Can someone help us with our luggage?" she asked, switching her little purse to her other arm and grinning a bit wider as Clare paled beside me.

Clare might not have known they were vampires, but I was beginning to realize that you didn't need to know someone was dangerous for your instincts to kick in and tell you that this certain someone was very bad news. That is, after all, what instincts are for.

"I can help you," I said quickly. I knew they were vampires, and I didn't happen to fear pretty much anything right now. I stepped quickly around the front desk, and then I was on the other side, grasping the smooth handles of their designer rollerboard luggage without even thinking. "Please follow me, ladies," I told them briskly, and then I was pacing quickly ahead of them down the hallway of portraits. I'd put them on the first floor, so at least I wouldn't have to deal with the stairs while trying to tug the luggage behind me.

I had no idea how the guests had gotten their luggage up to some of the higher floors without an elevator. It was quaint not to have one, and lent to the atmosphere of the Sullivan Hotel pretty well…but it wasn't exactly practical.

"Do I have this right—does the Conference begin this evening?" the blonde woman asked, pushing her own sunglasses up and onto the top of her head. The other woman said nothing as we walked down the corridor and kept her sunglasses on.

"Yes, you're right on schedule," I told them. I was glad Clare had told me that fact earlier.

"Wonderful!" the blonde woman, Magdalena, took a slim phone out of her alligator handbag and pressed its face, typing something into it.

The other woman, even though she was wearing sunglasses I couldn't exactly see through, seemed to be staring at me. I felt her gaze against me, and despite my earlier bravado, it was unnerving. I pressed my shoulders back and walked as quickly as I could toward the far door next to the spiral staircase. It had an old "Exit" sign lit overhead in a very retro font, and when I pushed open the door, holding it for the two women, the first floor room hall stretched on ahead of us, covered in a lush red carpet the exact same shade as drying blood.

I found their rooms, one thirteen and one fourteen, side by side. "Keep the change," said Magdalena once I'd gotten the bags inside each room and ducked outside with forced politeness.

She pressed a crisp, unfolded hundred-dollar bill into my hand, and then closed the door in my face with a wide smile.

Huh, I thought, staring down at my hand. Vampires are surprisingly good tippers. I could never have predicted that.

For a long moment I debated about folding the bill up and tucking it under my shirt and safely into my bra, because I had no other place to put it. But then I realized how close I was to the spiral stairs. It'd be the work of only a few moments to trot up them, deposit the money in my room, and then return to the front desk to continue helping Clare.

My mind wasn't really on the hundred-dollar bill—though it *was* nice—as I walked back down the hallway and began to make my way to my room. My thoughts turned, as always, to Kane. To Kane who'd leaned toward me as if she needed to be close to me. To Kane who had invaded my constant dreams, to Kane who I wanted to be with more than anything.

I breathed out brokenly and rounded the last bend of the spiral staircase...but I paused on the landing, gazing down the hallway to my room. A woman knelt in front of my door. She had short black hair, wore overalls and a plaid shirt, and—with a screwdriver—was fiddling with the lock of my door.

But that's not what made me pause.

Standing beside her, over her, as if supervising her actions with micromanaging precision, was a form I would be grateful to never see for the rest of my life. With her hands on her hips and her toe tapping, Melody stood tensely in her bright red dress, the scarlet fabric moving restlessly by her leg as she tapped her toe with aggravated, jerky motions.

Even though I hadn't made a sound, Melody straightened just then, and she turned to look down the hallway, her eyebrows raised as if she was surprised to see me at such an early hour.

But then that surprise faded almost immediately, and over her beautiful face a malicious glee began to spread as wide as her wickedly grinning mouth.

"Ah, Rose," she all but purred, crossing her arms in front of her chest as she chuckled a little. "You have perfect timing." She straightened to her full height and angled her chin up, looking down her nose at me as her words grew sharper. "Your suitcases have been taken down to the front desk."

Her final words were a knife in my heart, sharp and twisting:

"Your services at the Sullivan Hotel are no longer required."

...to be continued

Will Rose lose Kane forever to a woman who should never have returned? Experience this epic romance as it unfolds in the fourth Sullivan Vampire story, *Eternal Dance*, available now!

Acknowledgements

Being a writer is a lonely pursuit—you spend so much time in your head and in the worlds that you're writing that you really start to appreciate the people who stick with you and care about you even when you do crazy things like write until all hours of the morning and talk incessantly about your stories. So I am deeply and incredibly grateful for the loved ones in my life who put up with me and all of my eccentricities. You are loved and appreciated.

I can't believe the fans of this series—you guys are incredible and so supportive, and I'm overwhelmed that my vampires, who have lived in my head and in my computer files for so long, are being loved by you. Thank you for wanting to know what happens next. You keep me writing and inspire me so much by your enthusiasm, and I am so grateful for it.

R.M., to whom this book is dedicated, is one of the few people who never gave up on vampires, and she has never given up on me. Your friendship is one of the best things in my life, and this one's for you.

Em keeps things lively and entertaining and just a little scary and always reminds me to take breaks from my work.

K. has been reading and supporting and being endlessly enthusiastic about my work for as long as

I've been writing it, and I began writing vampires because she knew how much I loved them and told me I could do justice by them. I've never forgotten that, even all these years later. Thank you.

M. pushes me to be better, and is one of the most inspiring women I've ever met. Thank you for reading my stories and helping me be an even better writer through your encouragement and belief in me.

There are many more women (and a few guys, and surely a few cats) who inspire me, care about me and help me to be and write the best I'm capable of. I love you, and thank you.

Without the love of my life beside me, I would have no reason to tell stories or to see the beauty in this world. She is my foundation in everything and my reason for being. I love you.

Bridget Essex

Made in the USA
Lexington, KY
19 March 2016